# MARVEL MEOW

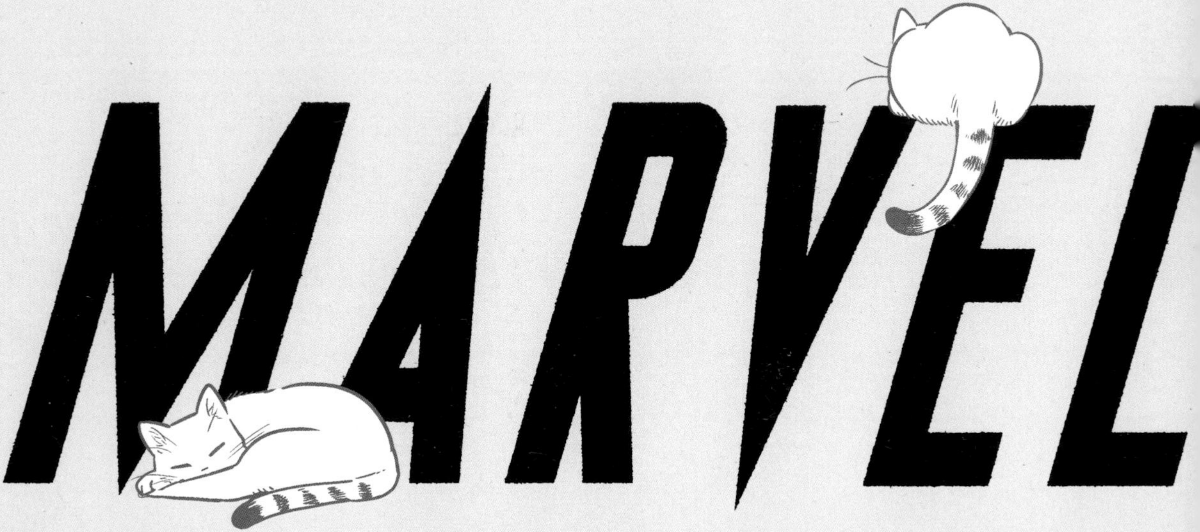
MARVEL

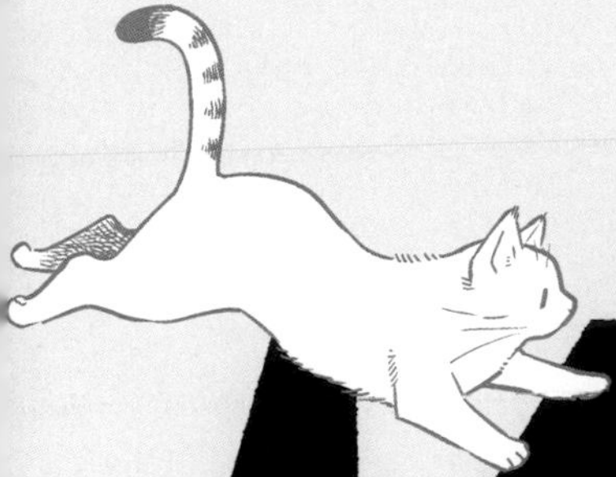

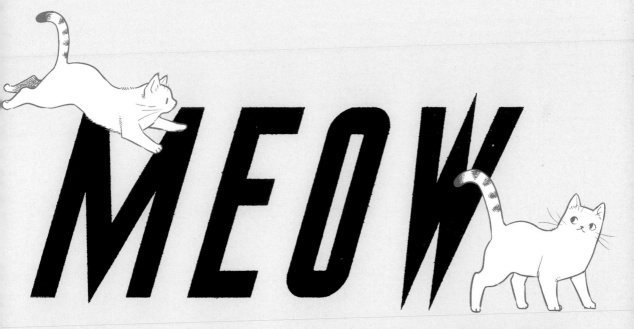

# MEOW

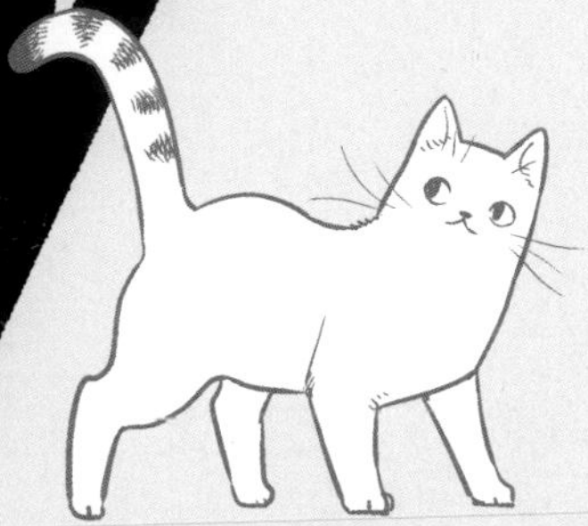

Nao Fuji

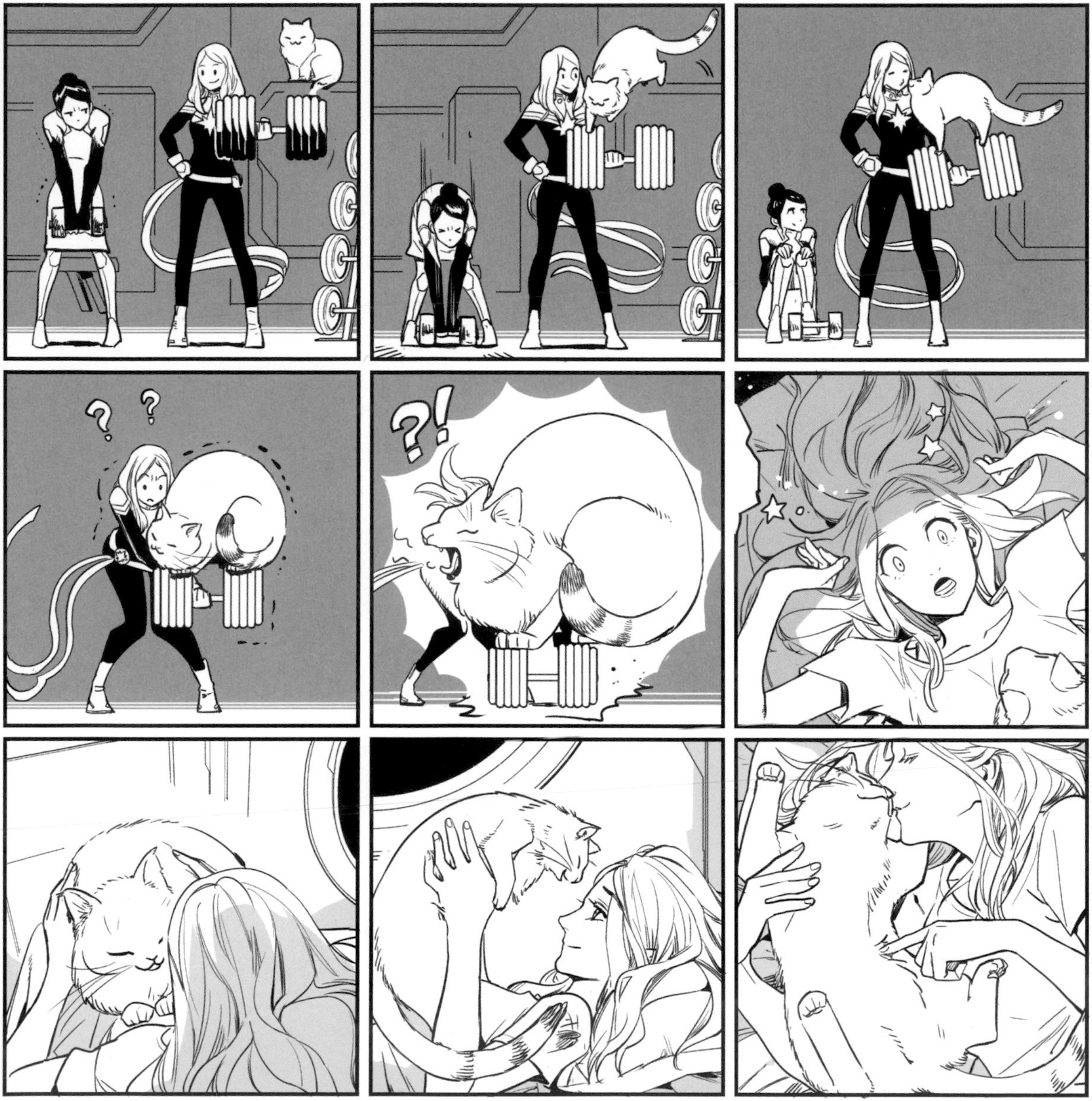
? ?
?!

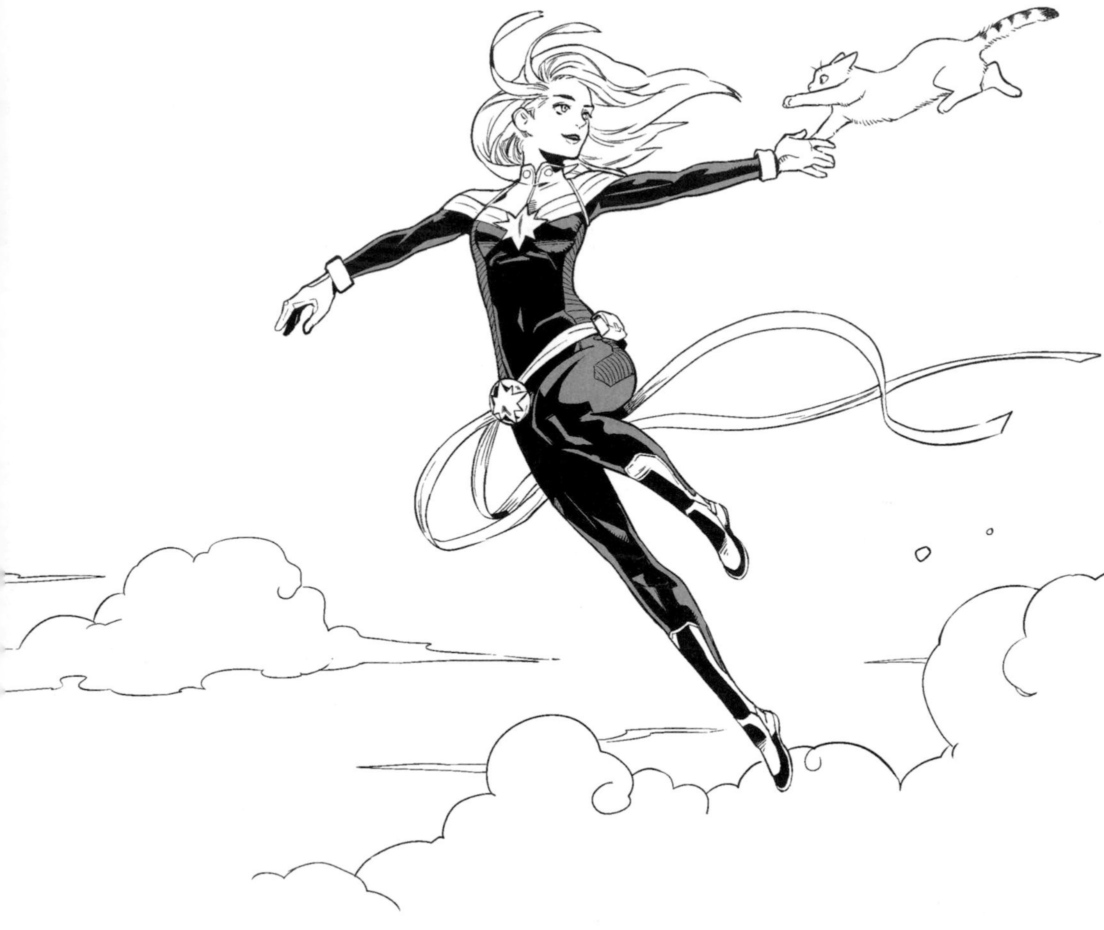

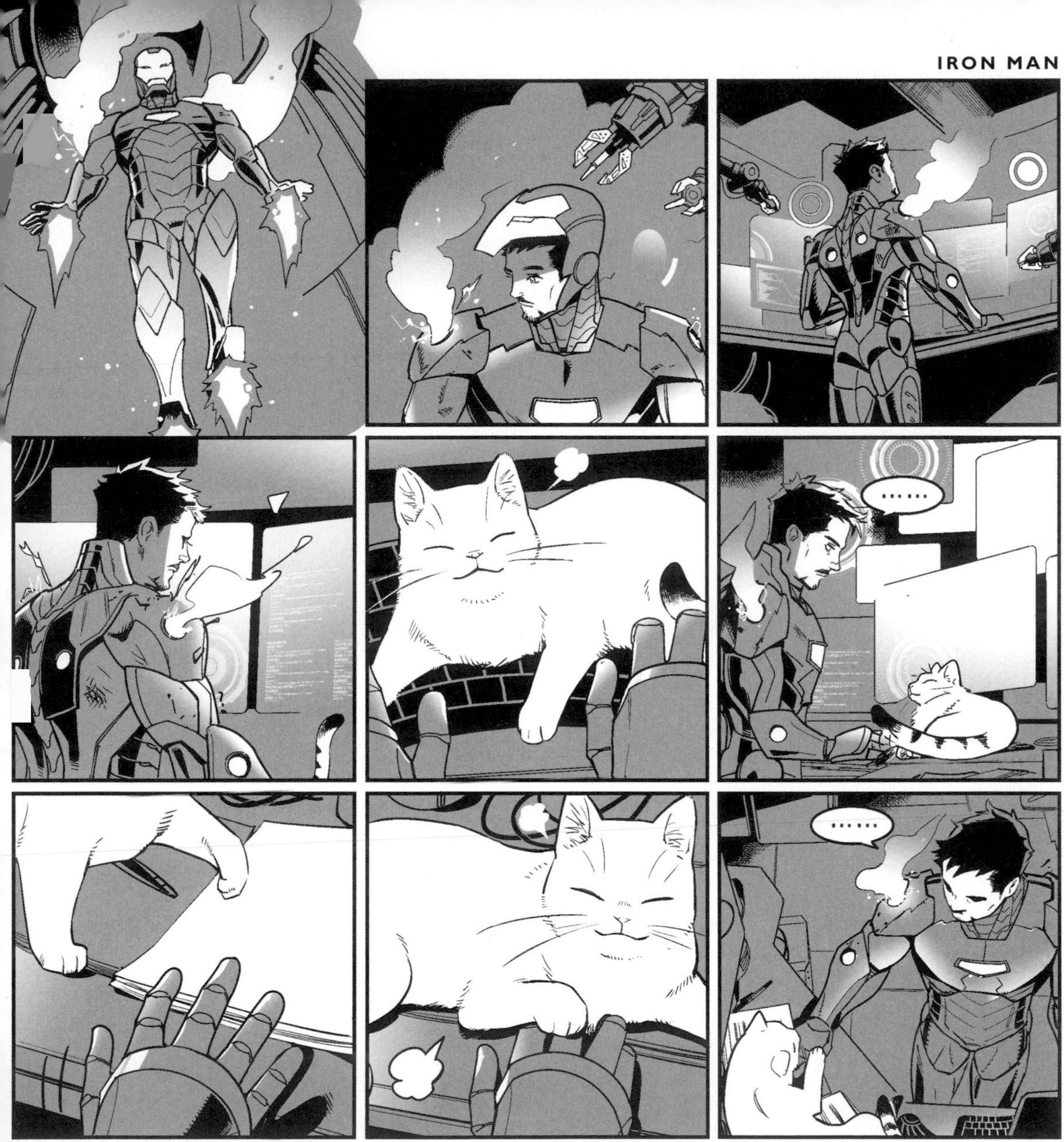
......
......

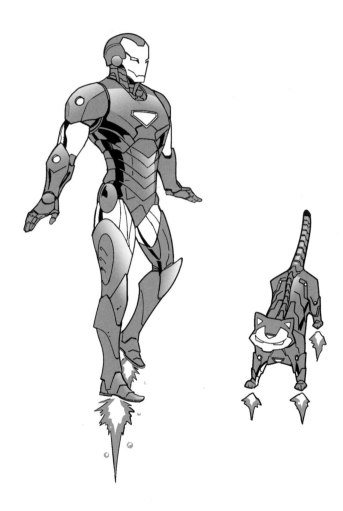

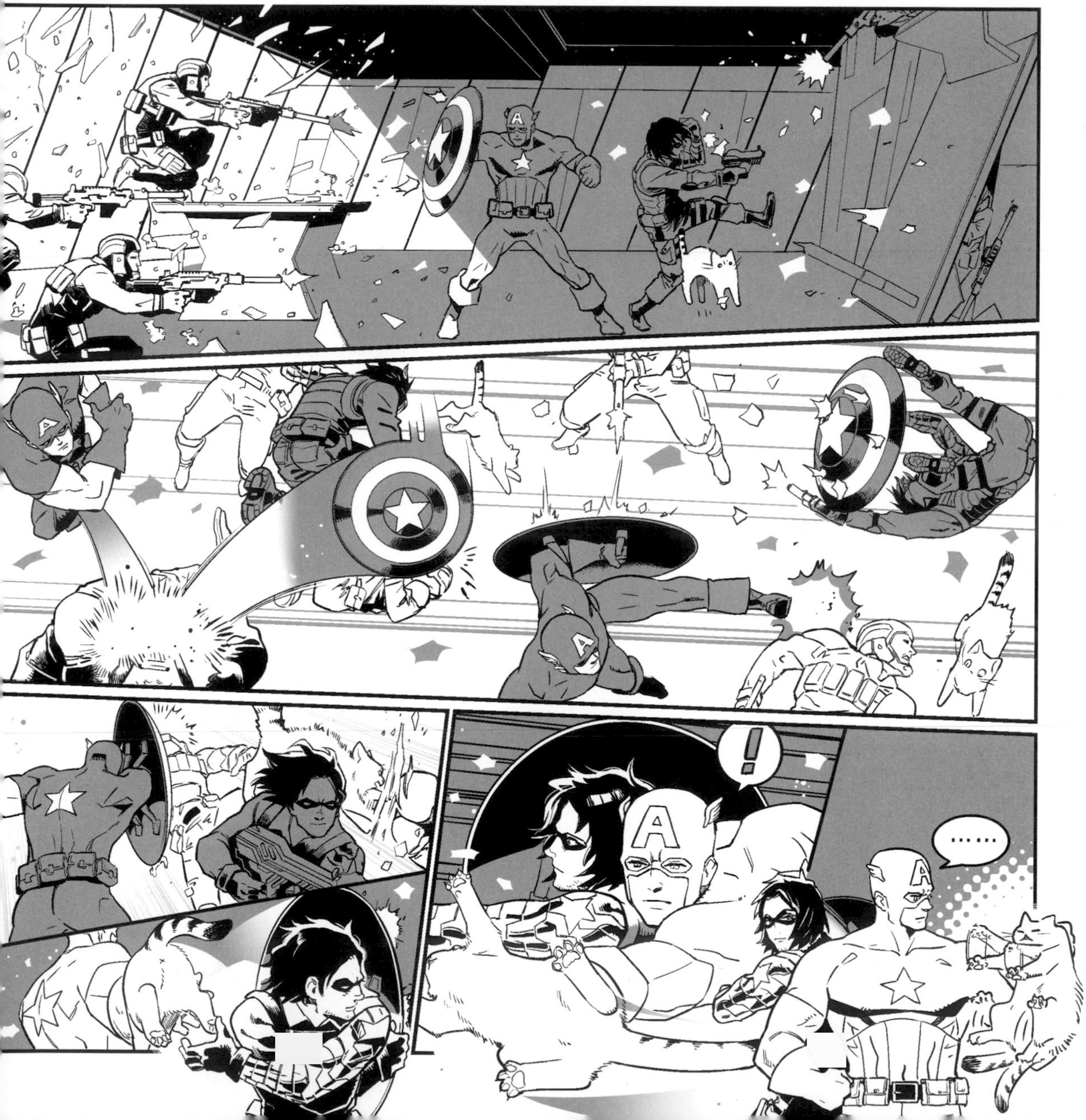
!
……

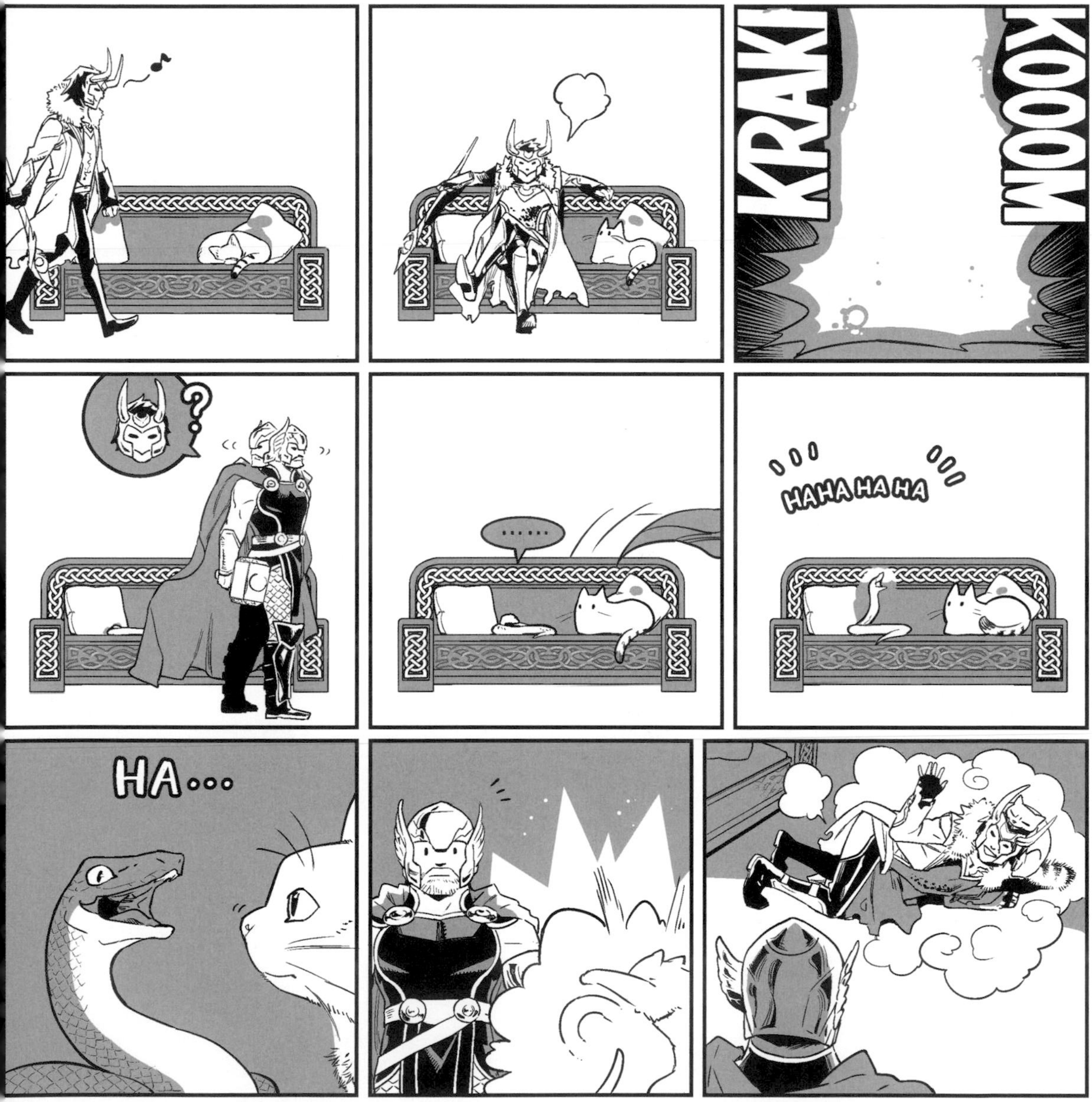
KRAKA
KOOOM
?
......
HAHAHAHA
HA...

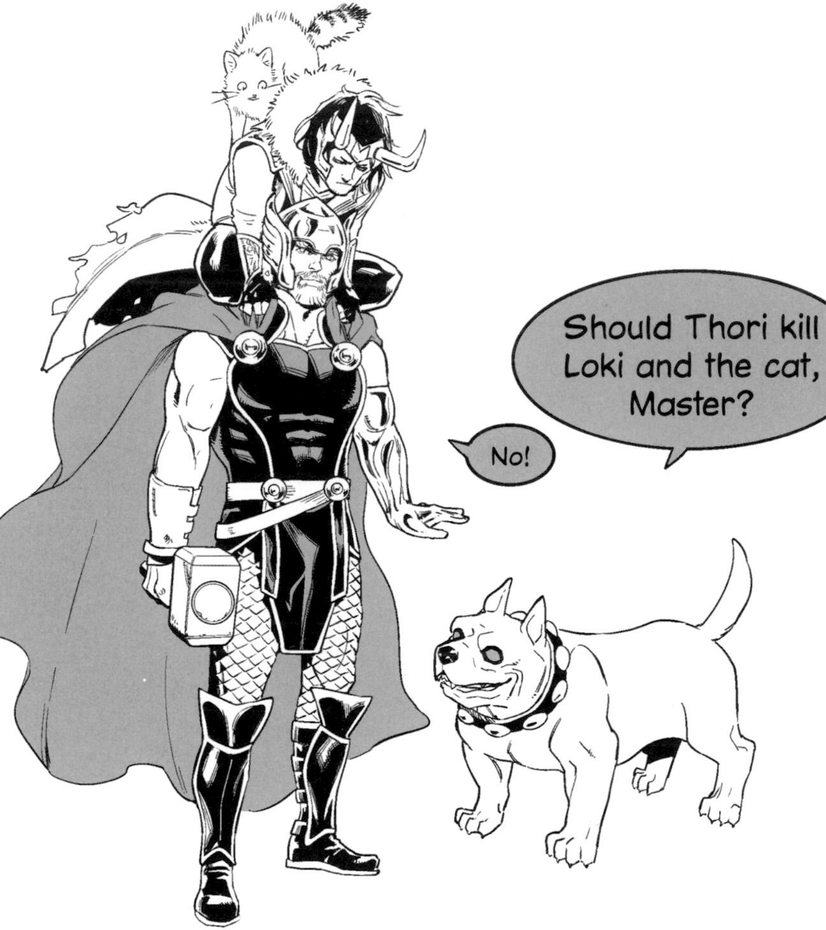
No!
Should Thori kill Loki and the cat, Master?

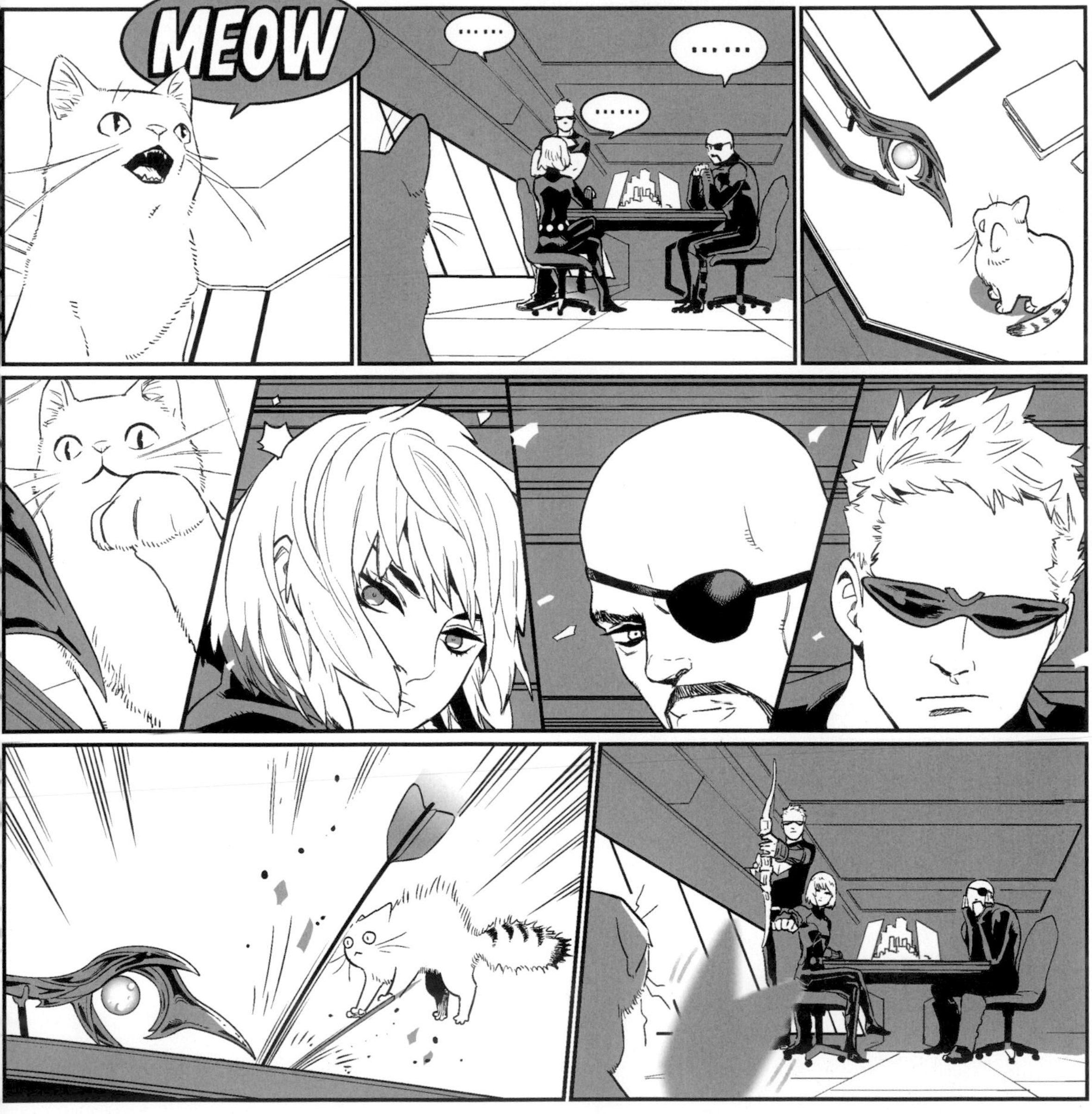
MEOW
......
......
......

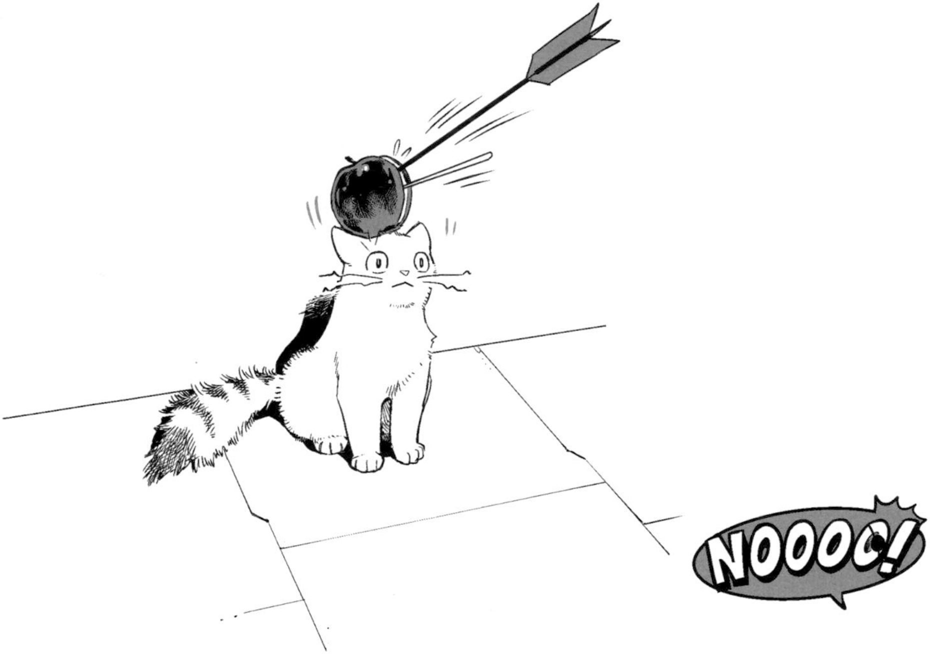
NOOOC!

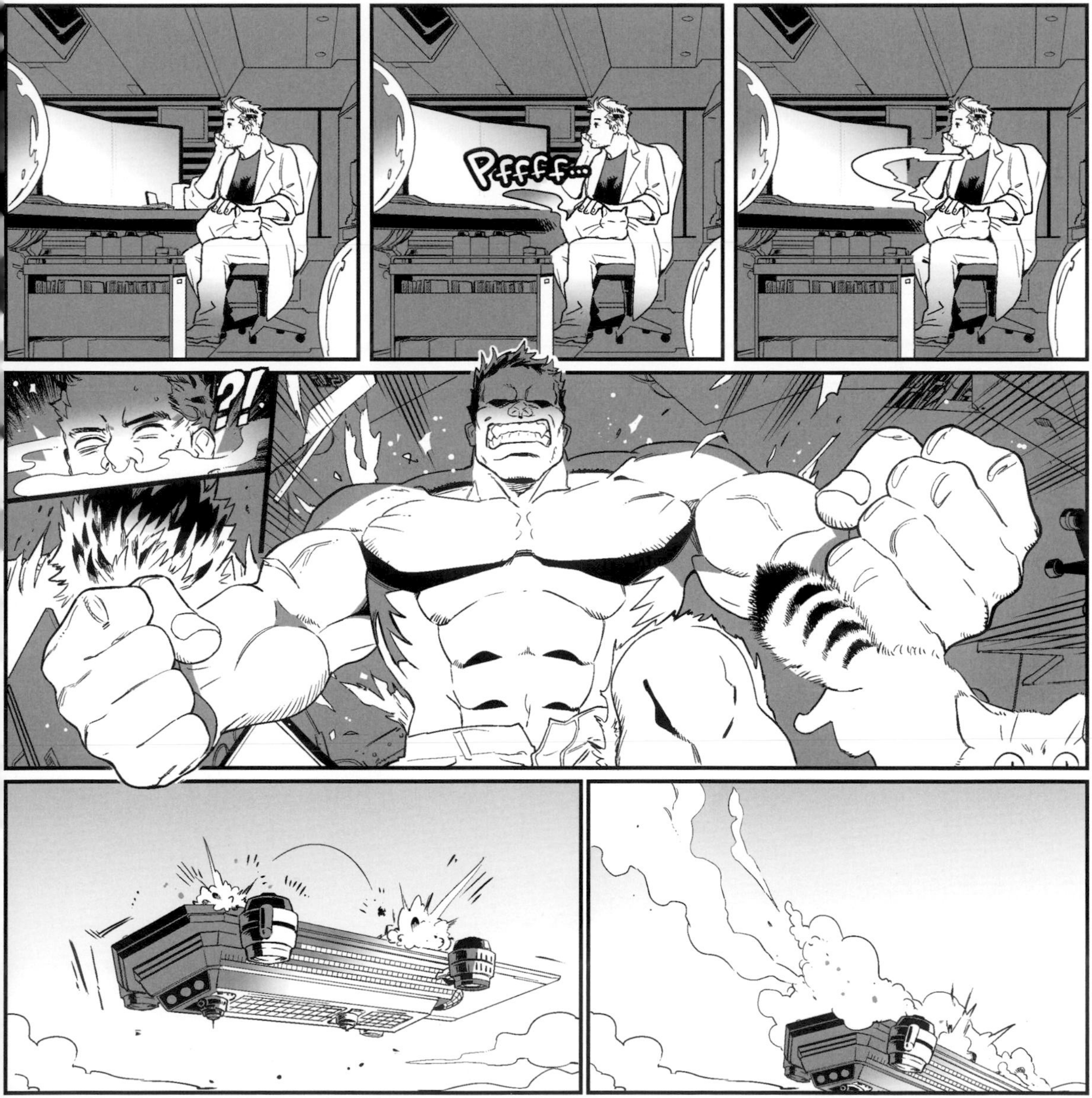
Pffff...
?!

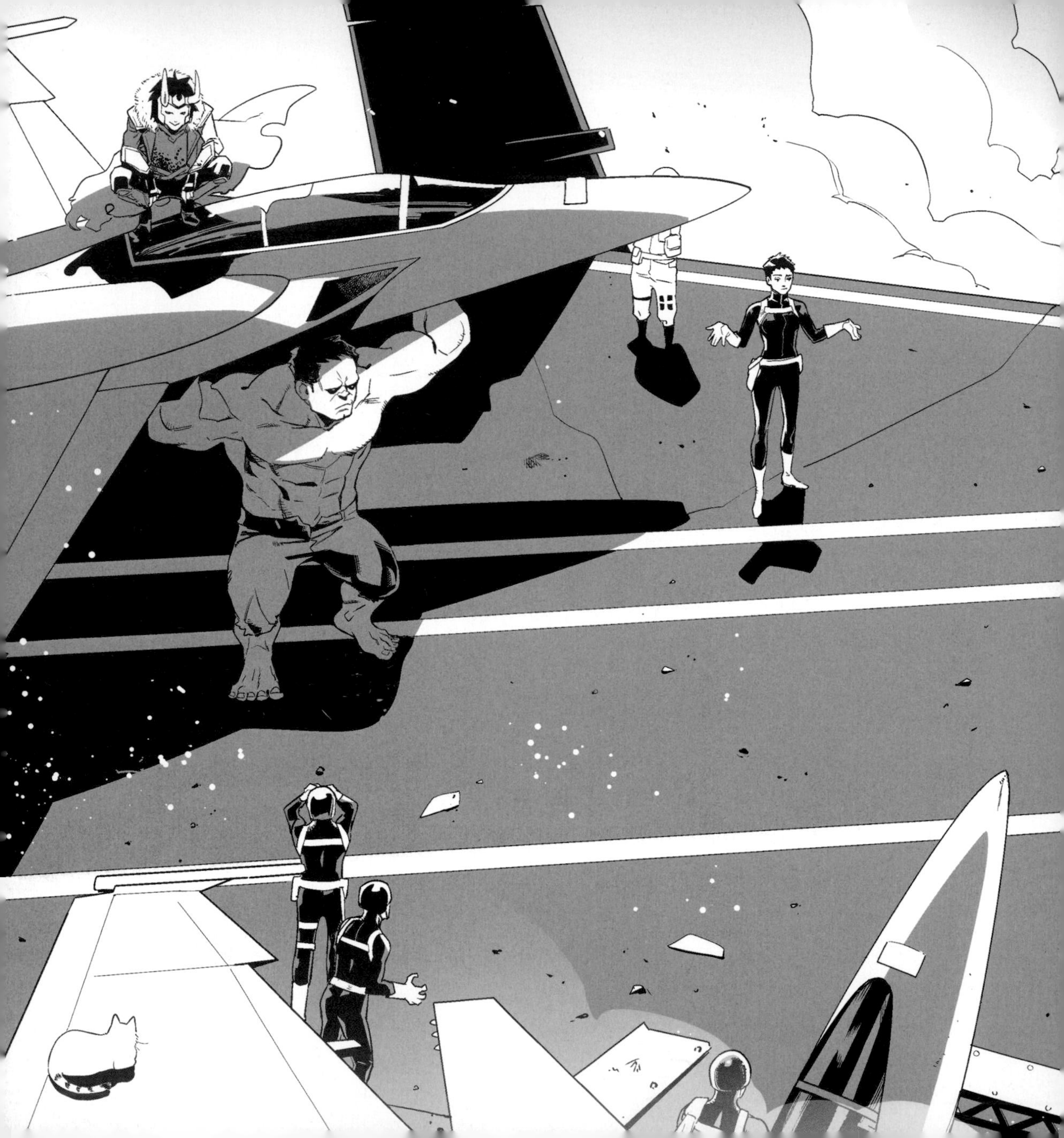

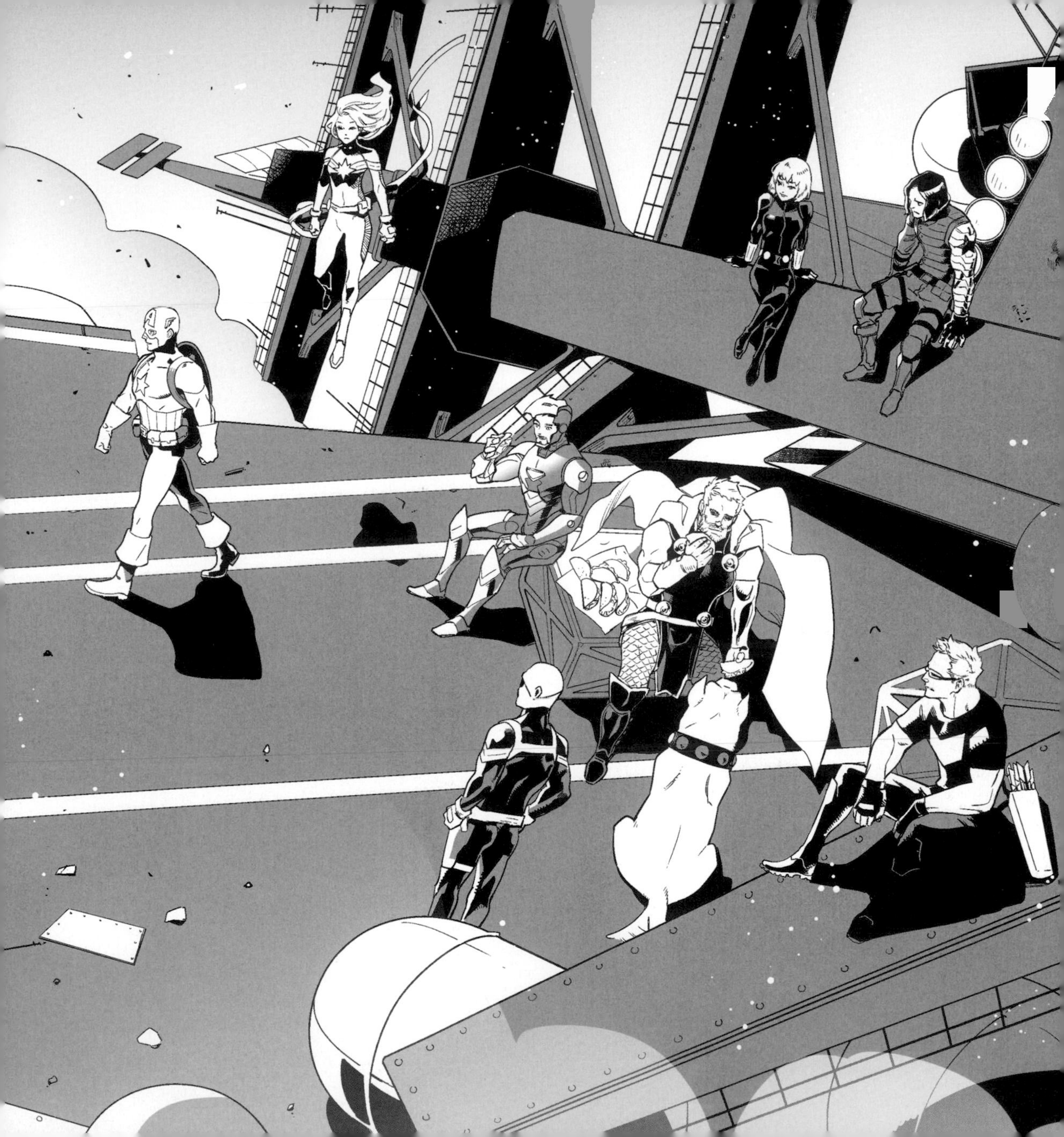

# CHARACTER PROFILES

## CHEWIE
Captain Marvel's pet flerken, an extraterrestrial that looks like a cat.

## CAPTAIN MARVEL —— P5
Carol Danvers. She gained her superhuman strength and powers of flight from the Kree, an alien race. The person next to her is her human assistant, Wendy Kawasaki.

## IRON MAN —— P7
Tony Stark, a genius inventor and a billionaire who fights in armor he created.

## CAPTAIN AMERICA —— P9
His physical body has been enhanced to the limits of human abilities by the Super-Soldier Serum.

## BUCKY BARNES —— P9
Also known as the Winter Soldier. He was Captain America's partner during World War II.

## THOR —— P11
The Norse god of thunder. He lives in Asgard.

## LOKI —— P11
Thor's adopted brother. As the god of mischief, he can transform himself into any living thing to deceive others.

## THORI —— P12
Thor's pet Hel-Hound. This vicious but loyal guard dog once belonged to Loki.

## HAWKEYE —— P13
A master of archery.

## BLACK WIDOW —— P13
A skilled spy trained in Russia.

## NICK FURY —— P13
Director of the intelligence agency S.H.I.E.L.D.

## HULK —— P15
When genius scientist Bruce Banner becomes angry, he transforms into the Hulk—the strongest hero there is!

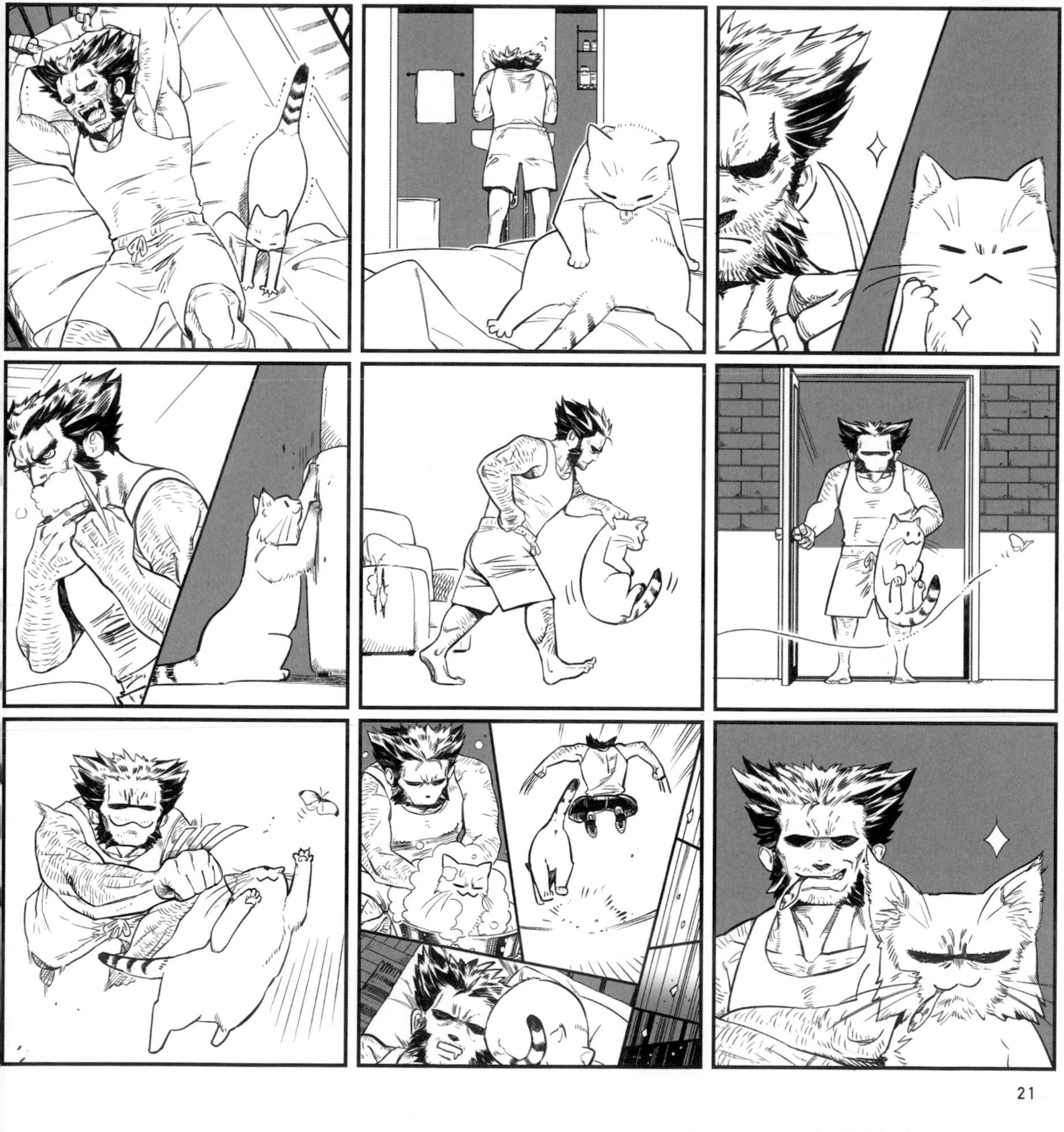

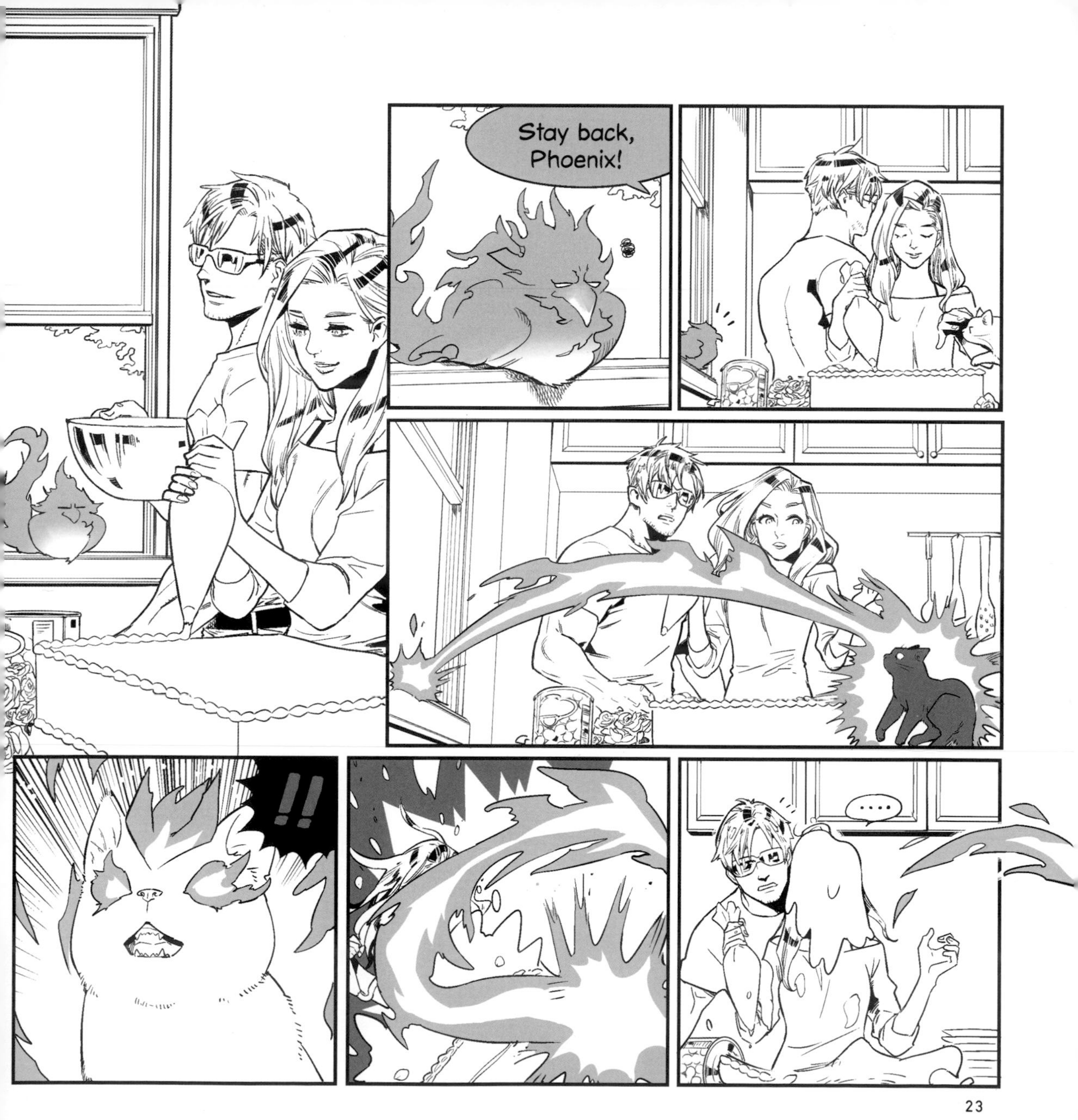
Stay back, Phoenix!
!!
....

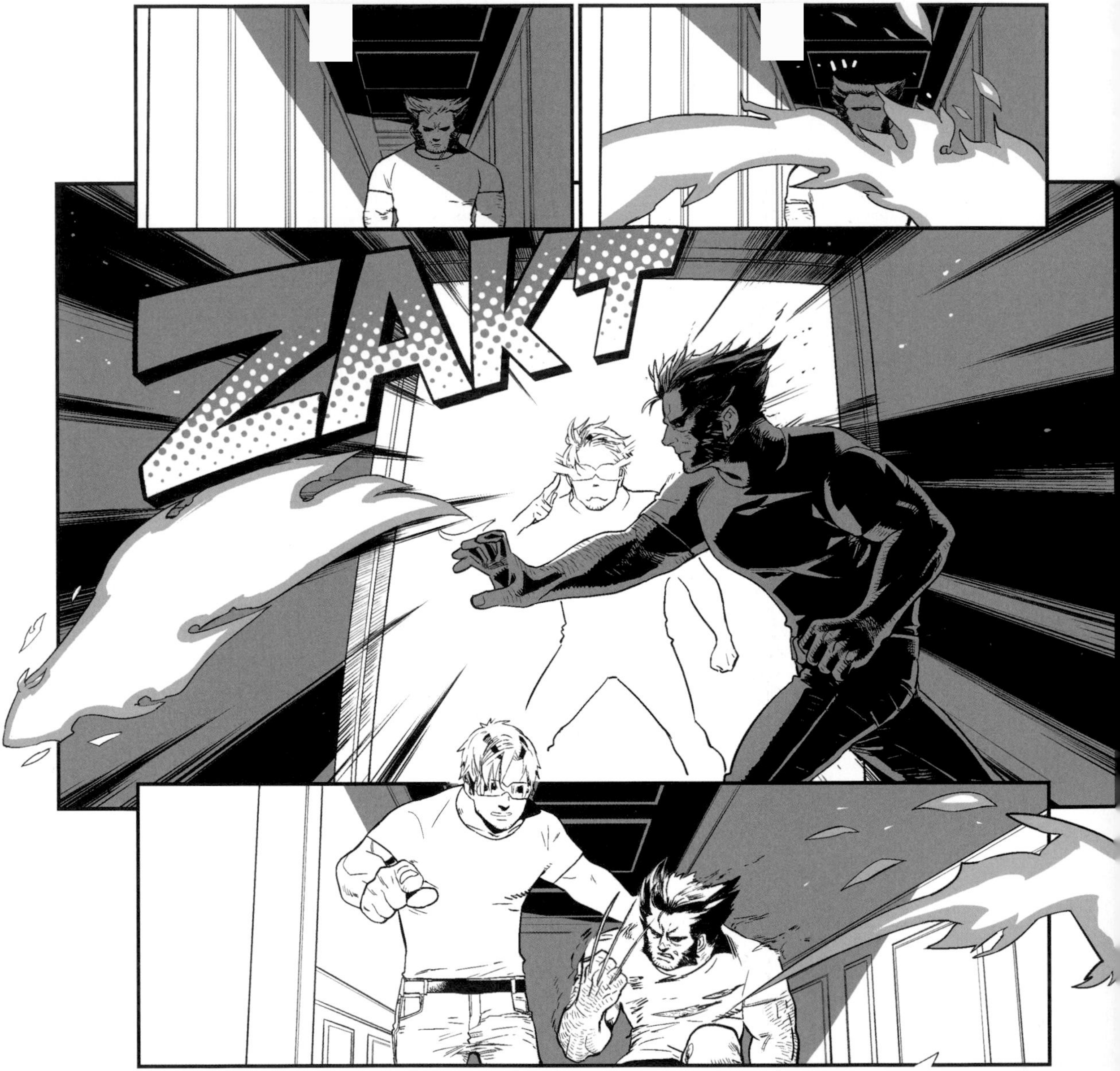
ZAKT

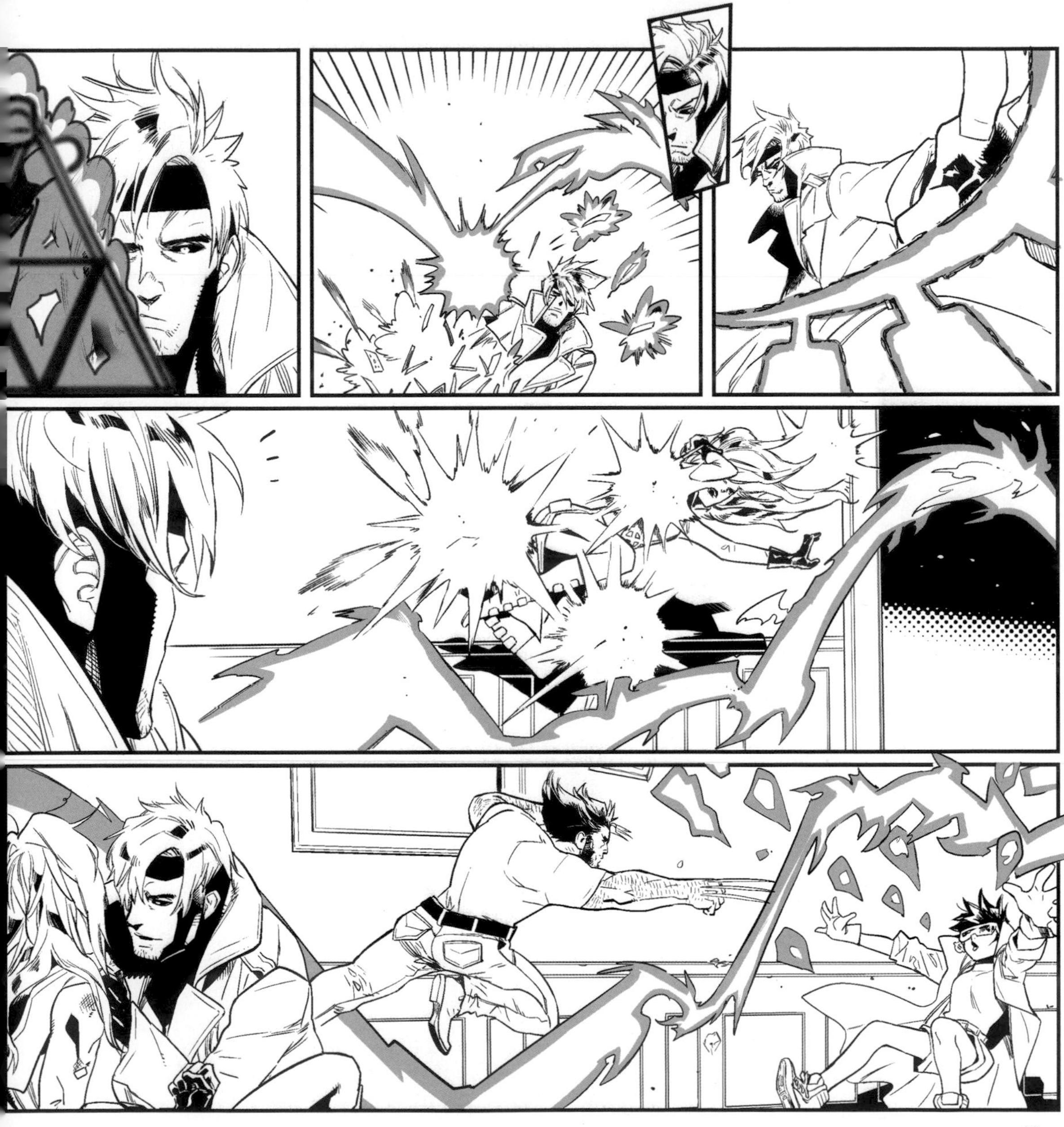

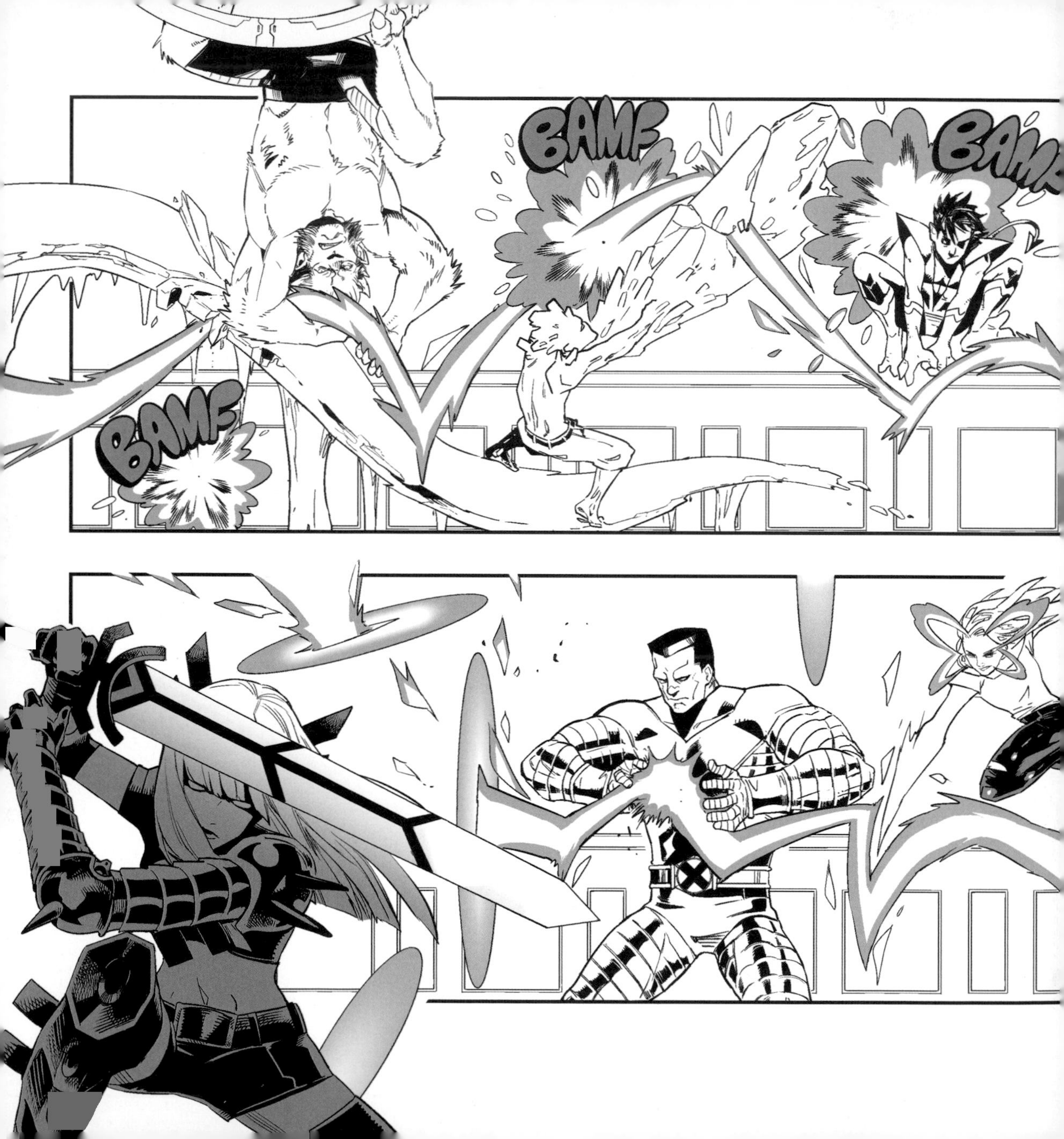
BAMF
BAMF
BAMF

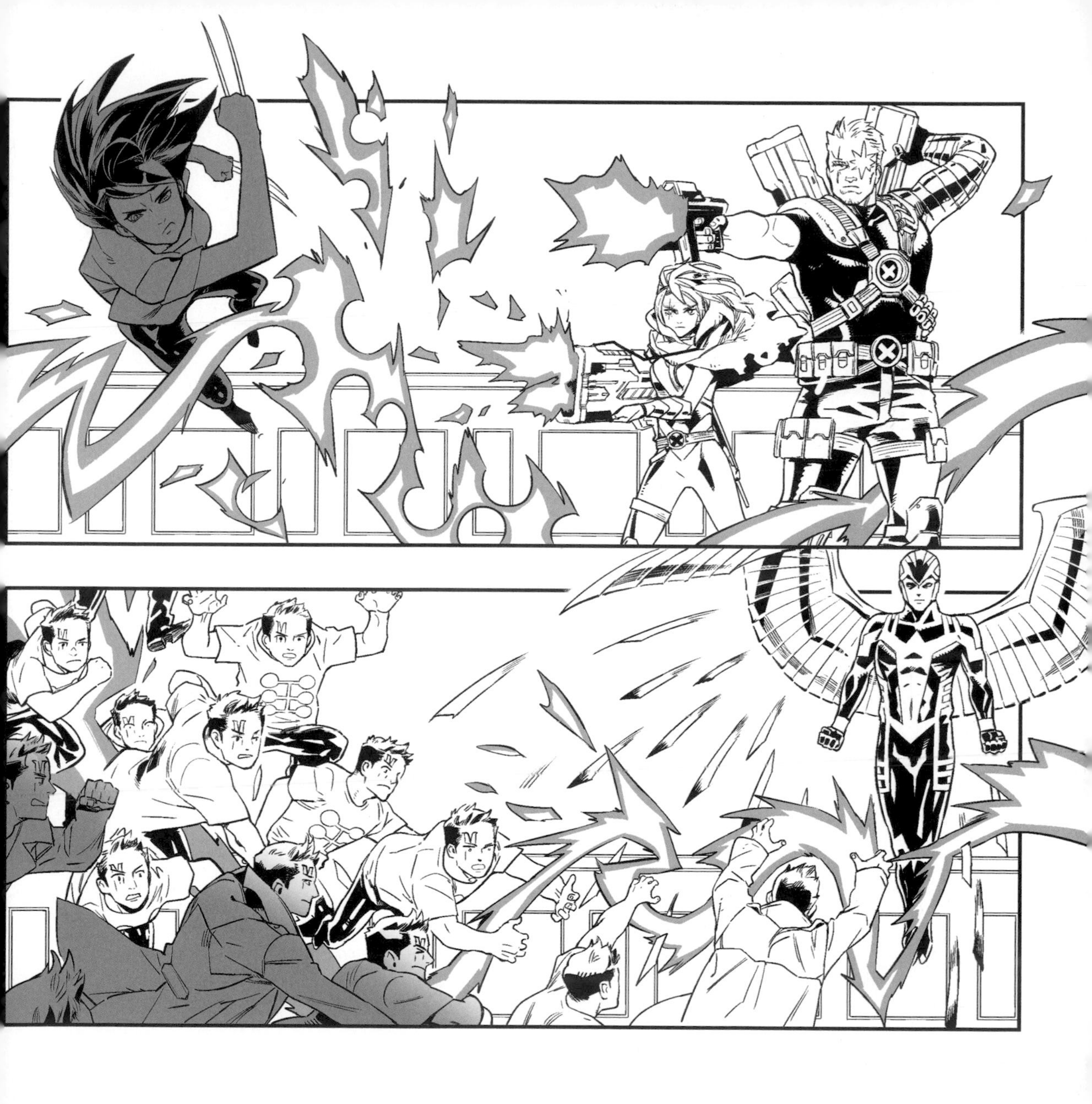

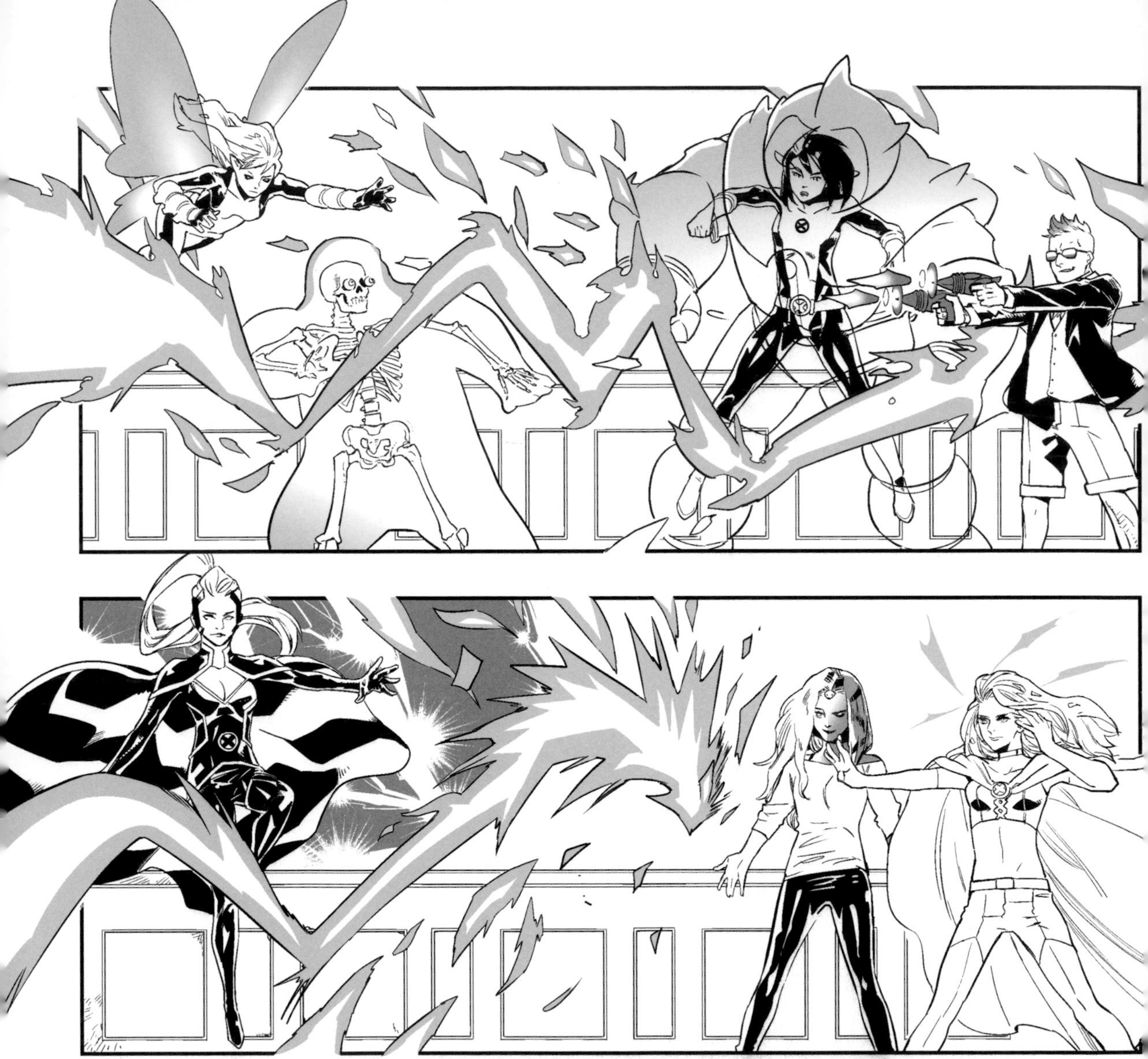

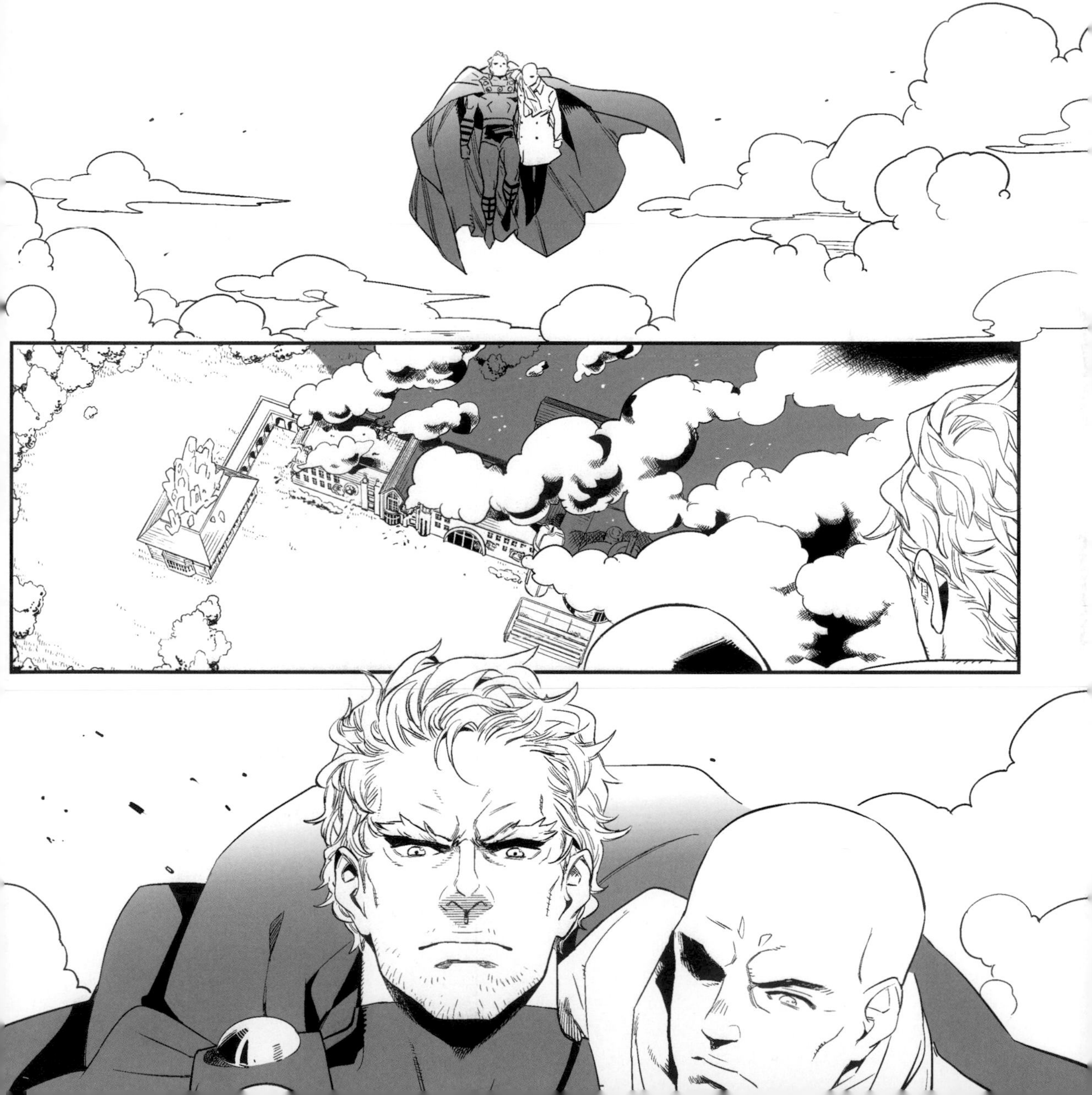

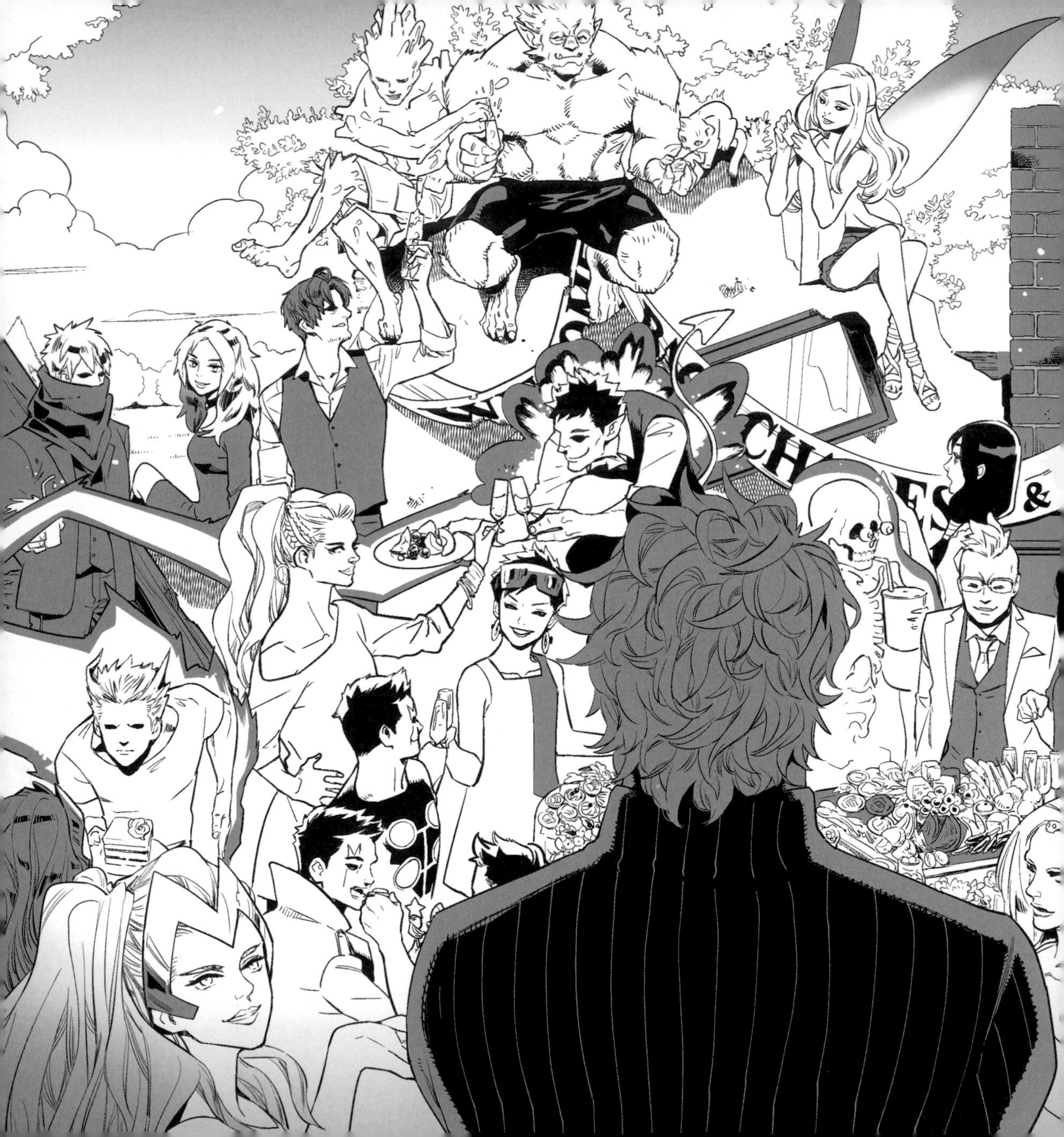

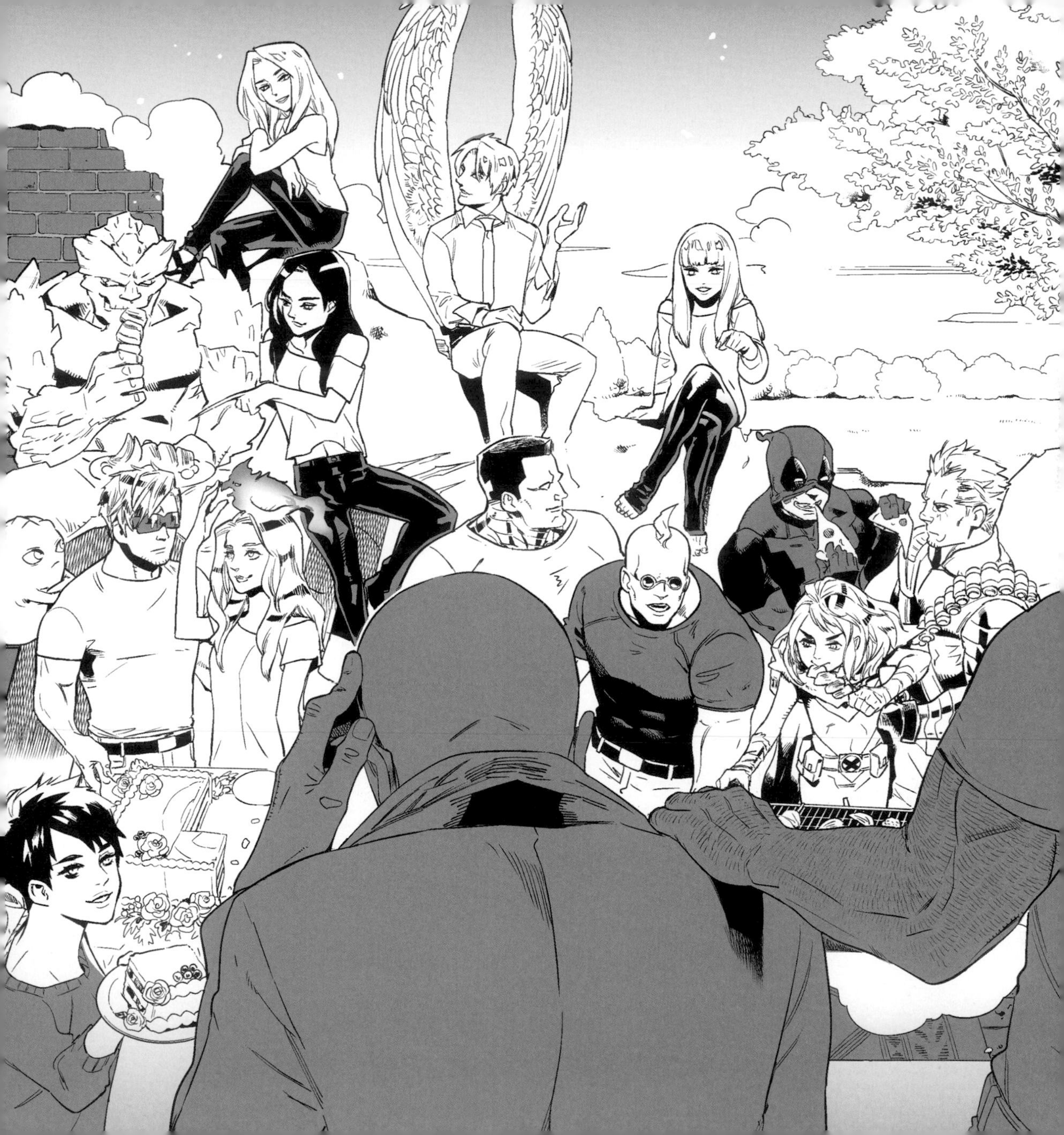

## CHARACTER PROFILES

### X-MEN

**WOLVERINE** — P21
His skeleton is reinforced with the indestructible metal alloy Adamantium. He uses the claws extending from his hands as weapons.

**JUBILEE** — P22
Can generate pyrotechnic energy blasts. She admires Wolverine.

**CYCLOPS** — P23
Fires powerful beams from his eyes.

**JEAN GREY** — P23
A telepath with telekinetic powers. She once hosted the Phoenix Force.

**PHOENIX** — P23
An immortal cosmic entity capable of destroying planets.

**GAMBIT** — P25
Has the ability to create and control kinetic energy. He charges objects such as cards with that energy and throws them with incredible skill.

**ROGUE** — P25
Absorbs the abilities and memories of those she touches. She is married to Gambit.

**BEAST** — P26
Possesses both genius intellect and superhuman strength.

**ICEMAN** — P26
Manipulates ice by freezing his own body or water vapor in the air.

**NIGHTCRAWLER** —— P26
Able to teleport by passing through an alternate dimension.

**MAGIK** —— P26
Wields the magical Soulsword and can teleport through space and time by opening disk-shaped portals.

**COLOSSUS** —— P26
Can transform his body into organic steel. He is Magik's older brother.

**PSYLOCKE** —— P26
Wields a telekinetic katana that she generates with her telepathic powers.

**X-23** —— P27
A clone of Wolverine. Her real name is Laura Kinney.

**CABLE** —— P27
A warrior born from Cyclops and a clone of Jean Grey and raised in the future of an alternate timeline.

**HOPE SUMMERS** —— P27
She was adopted by Cable and raised as the mutant messiah.

**MULTIPLE MAN** —— P27
Can instantly make copies of himself.

**ARCHANGEL** —— P27
He has also been the super hero known as Angel. He has an enhanced body and metal wings.

**PIXIE** —— P28
A winged mutant who can fly and wield magic.

**GLOB HERMAN** —— P28
His skeleton and internal organs float in bio-paraffin, a form of flammable living wax.

**ARMOR** —— P28
A mutant whose power is generating a psionic exoskeleton that gives her special abilities.

**QUENTIN QUIRE** —— P28
Also known as Kid Omega. He can manifest firearms just by thinking about them.

**STORM** —— P28
Has the ability to control the weather.

**MYSTIQUE** —— P28
Able to precisely mimic the appearance and voice of another person.

**EMMA FROST** —— P28
A telepath who can transform her body into a diamond form.

**PROFESSOR X** —— P29
Charles Xavier, the founder of Xavier's School for Gifted Youngsters and a powerful telepath.

**MAGNETO** —— P29
A charismatic man with the power to manipulate magnetic fields. He works toward the advancement of mutants. He is both an old friend and an enemy of Professor X.

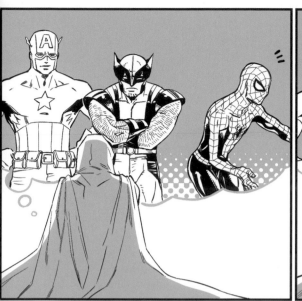

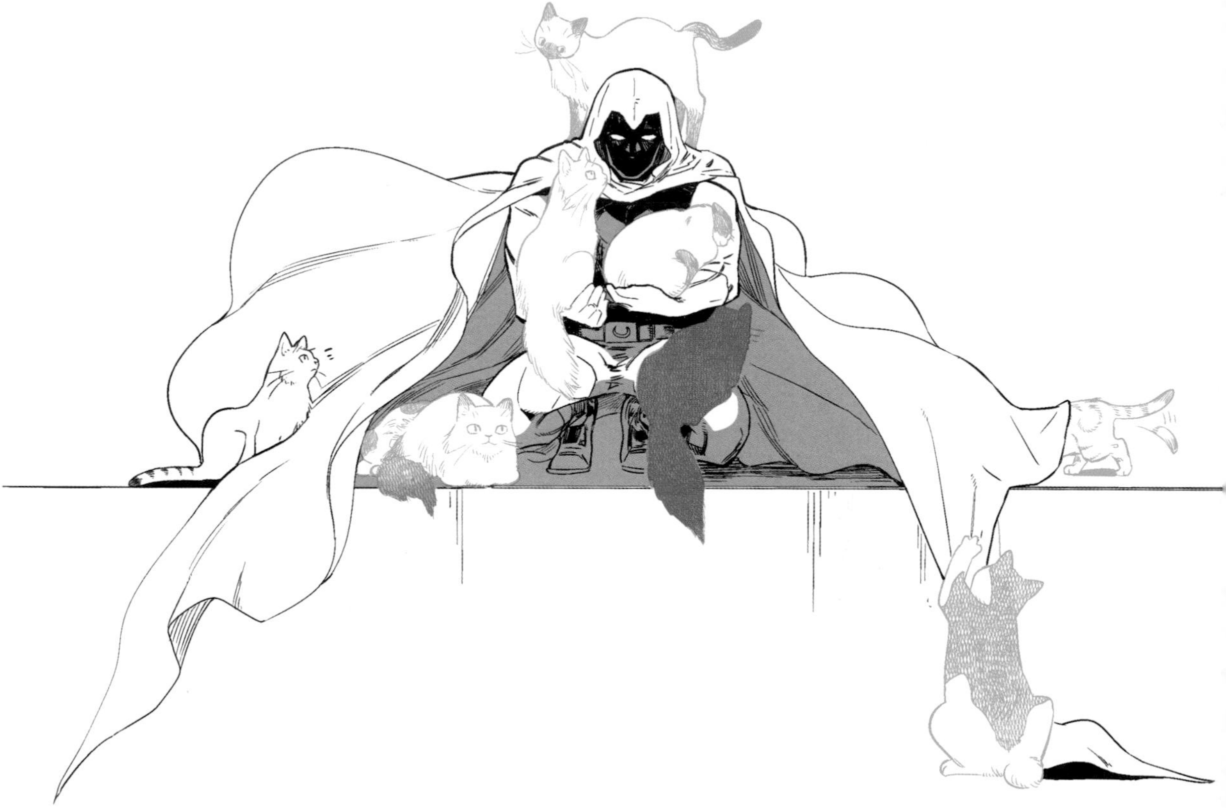

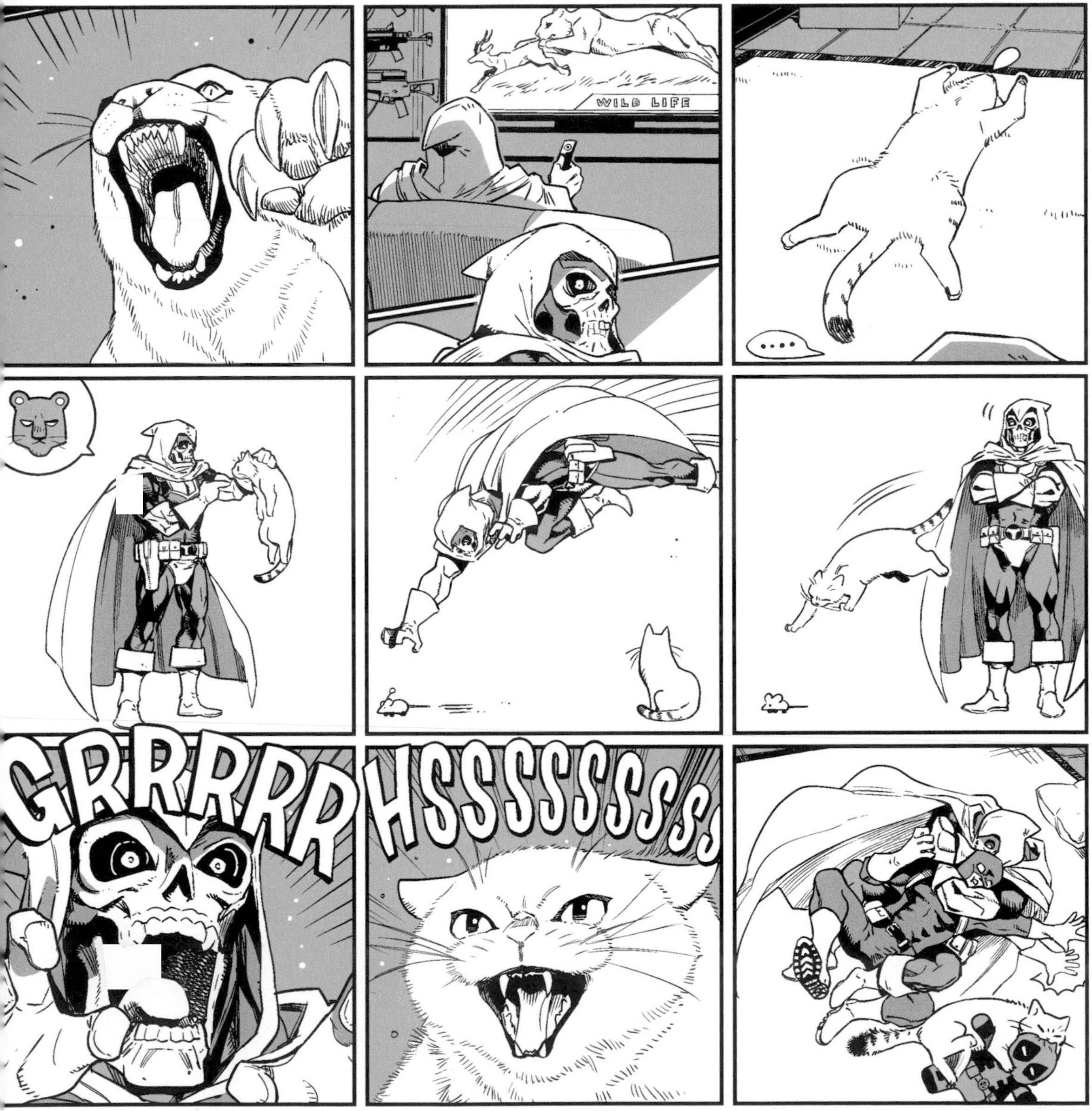
WILD LIFE
....
GRRRRRR
HSSSSSSSS

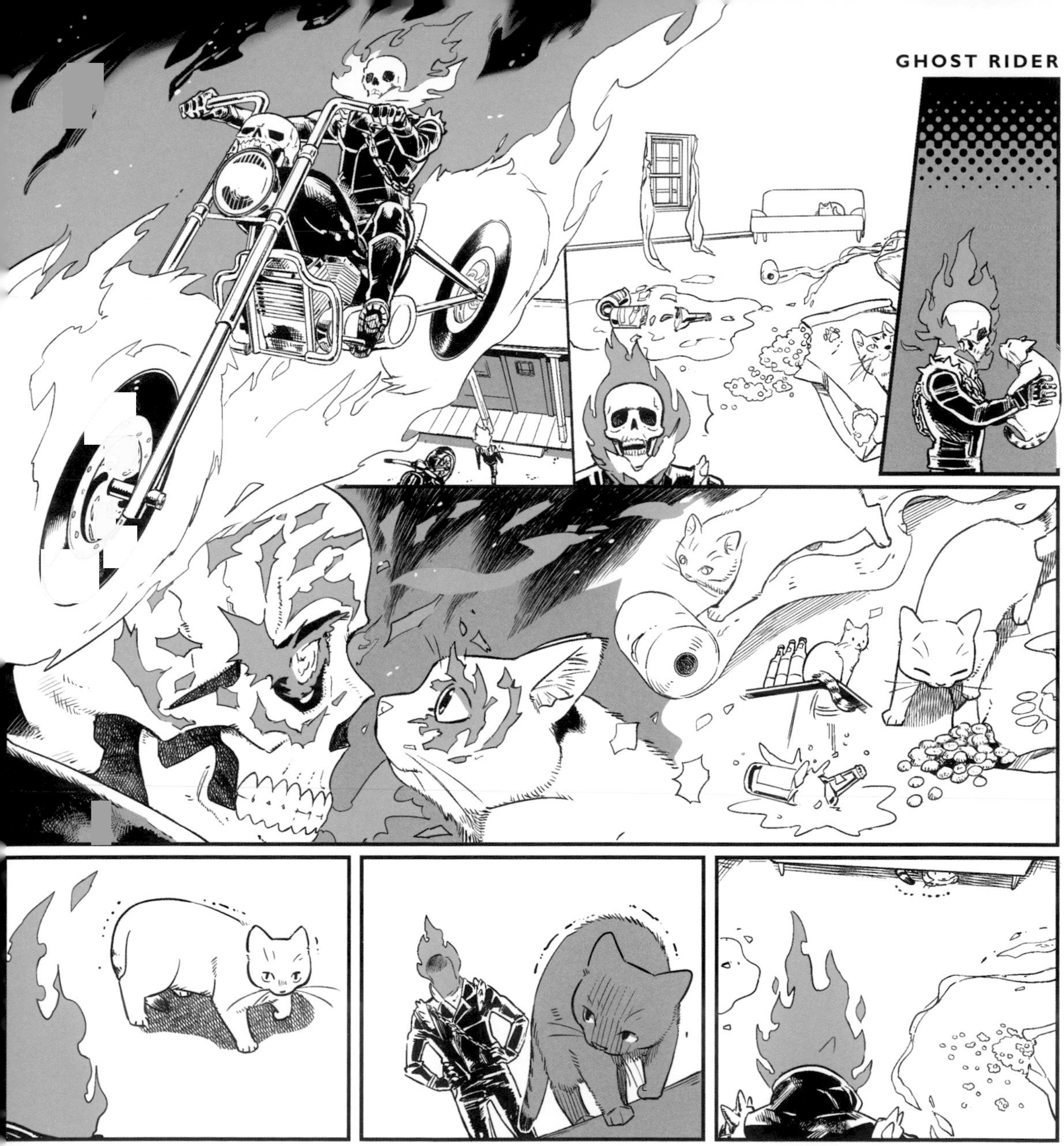

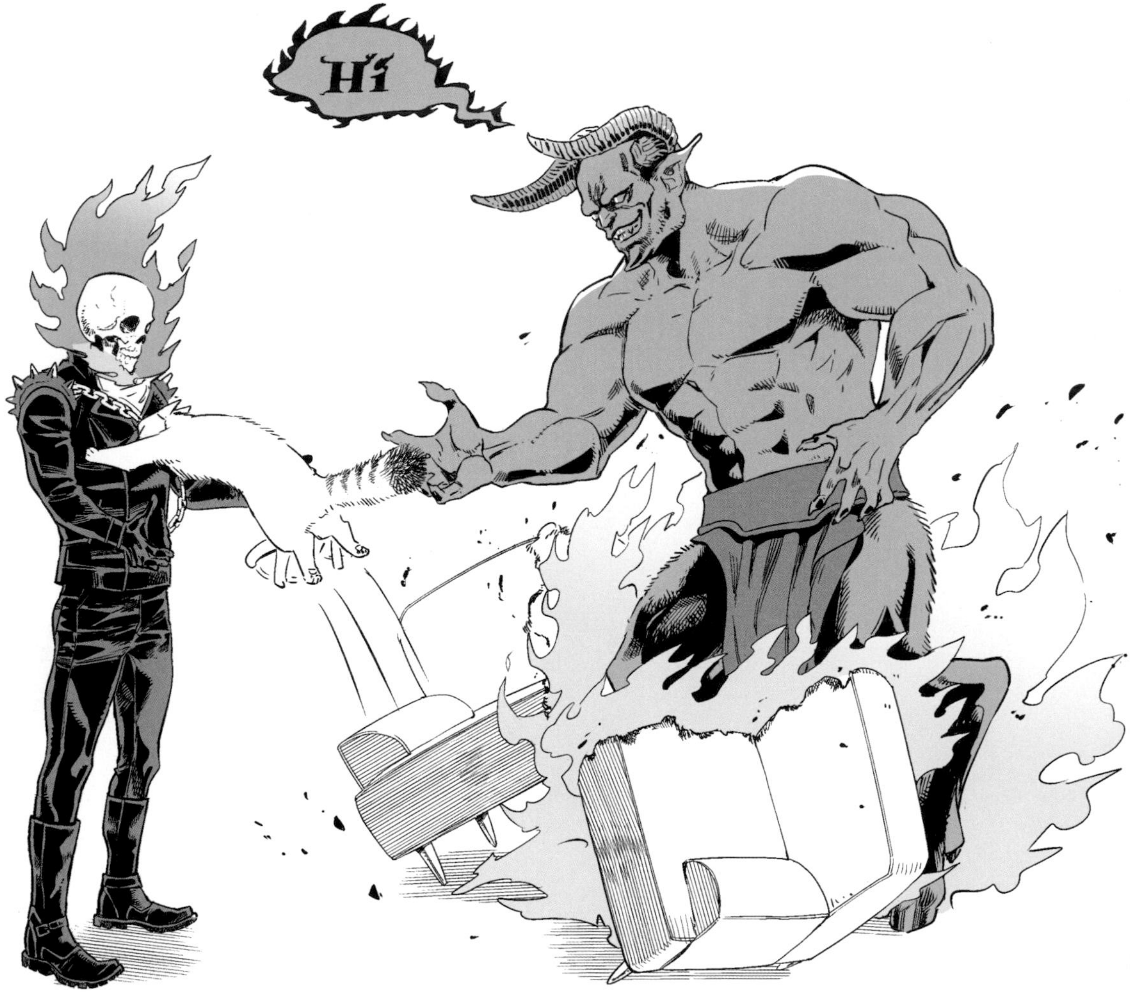
Hi

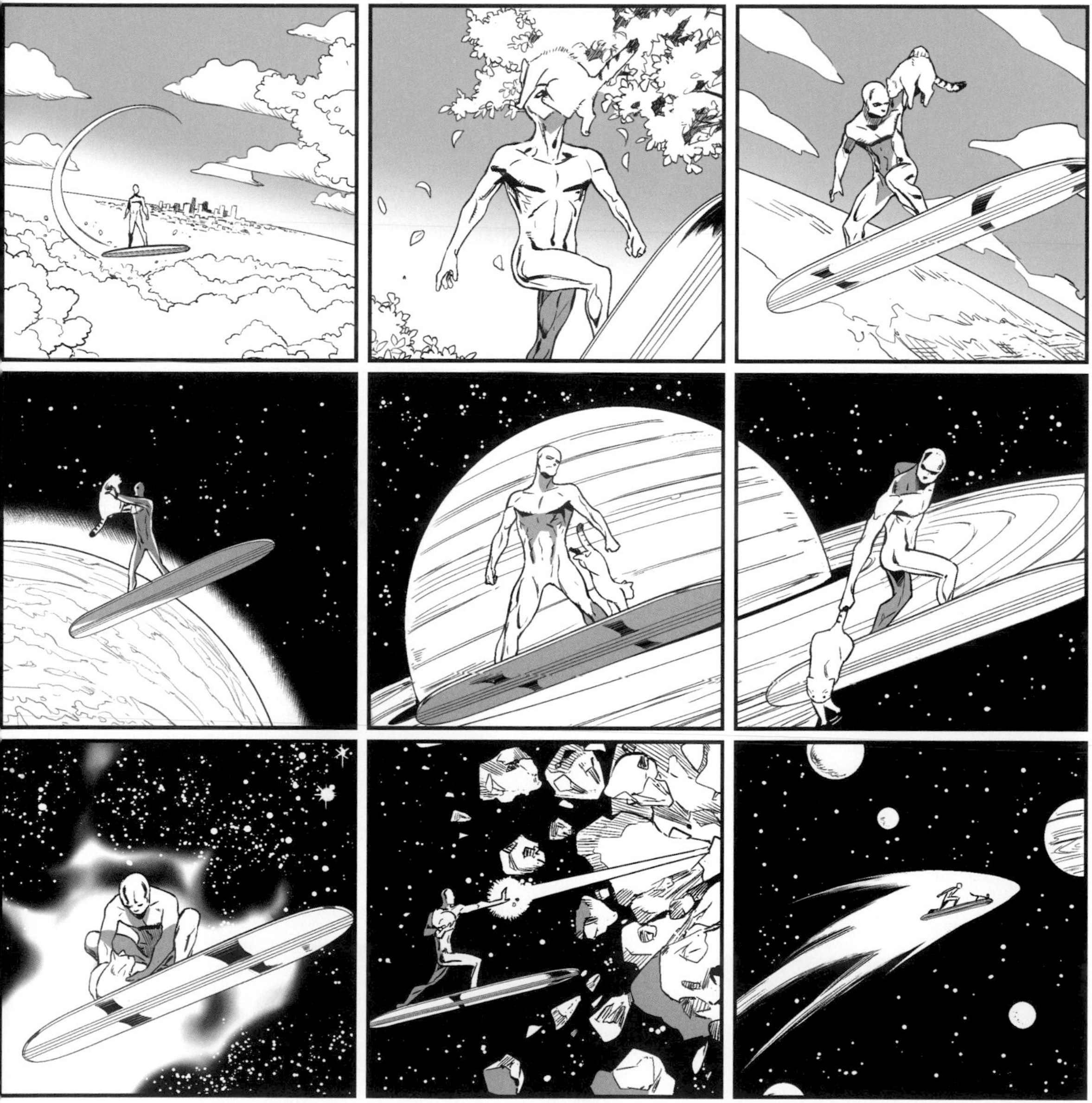

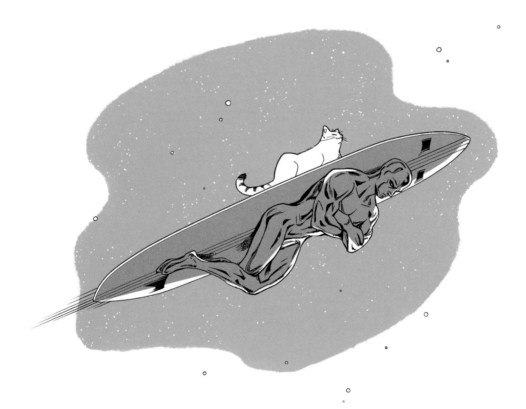

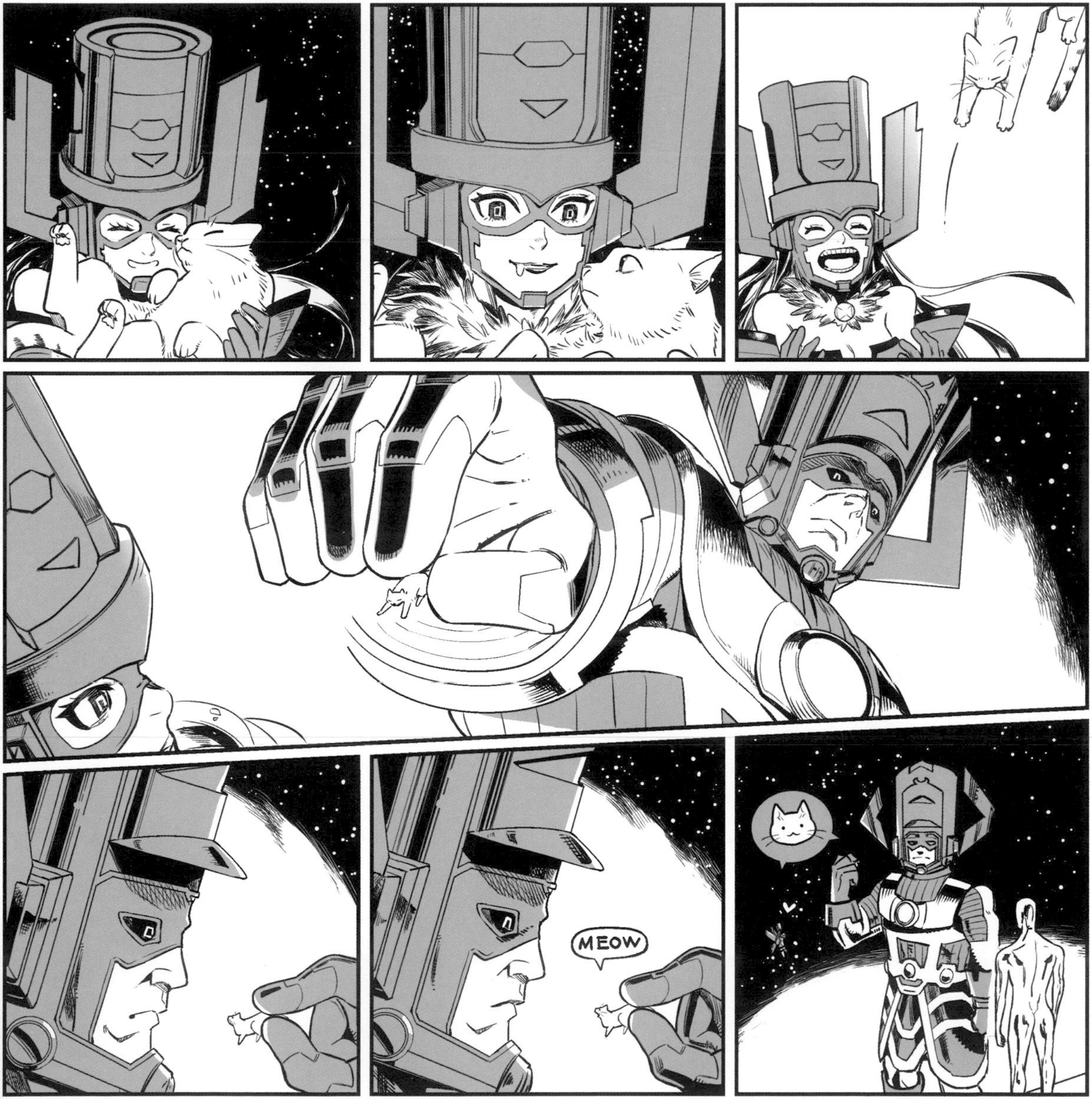
MEOW

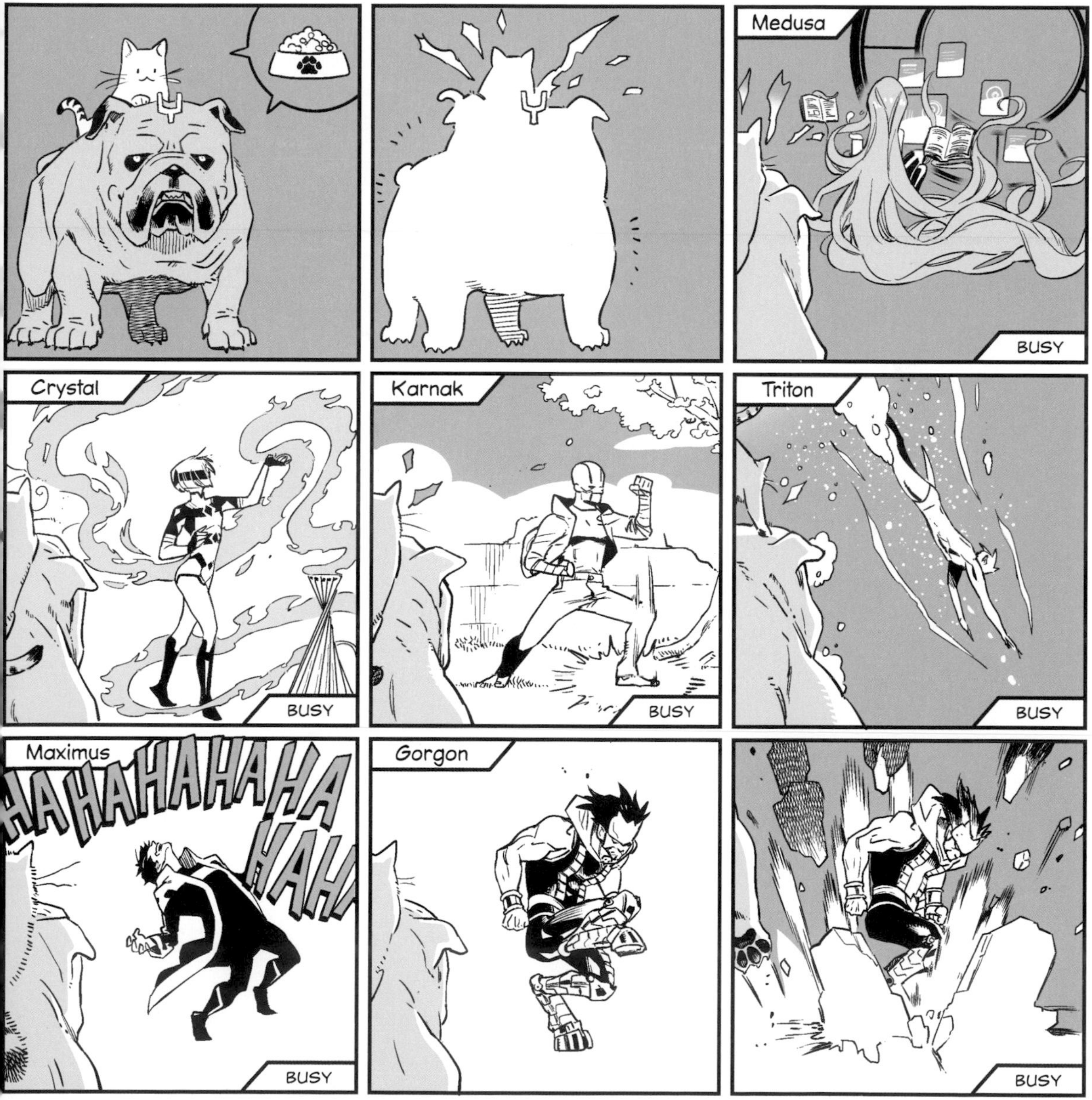
Medusa
BUSY
Crystal
BUSY
Karnak
BUSY
Triton
BUSY
Maximus
HAHAHAHAHAHA
HAHA
BUSY
Gorgon
BUSY

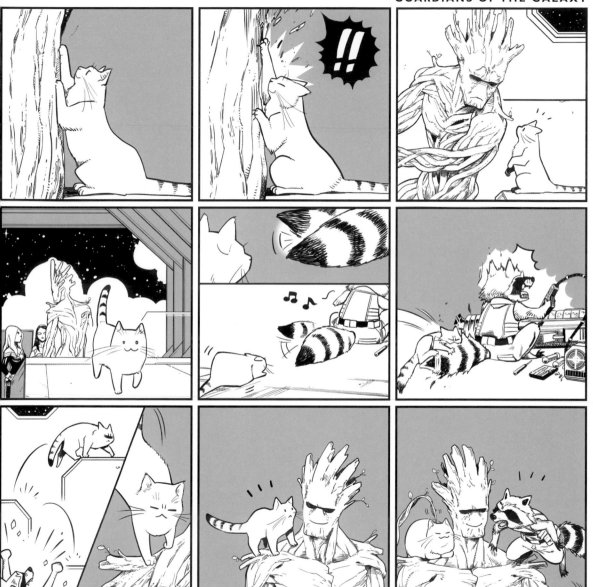

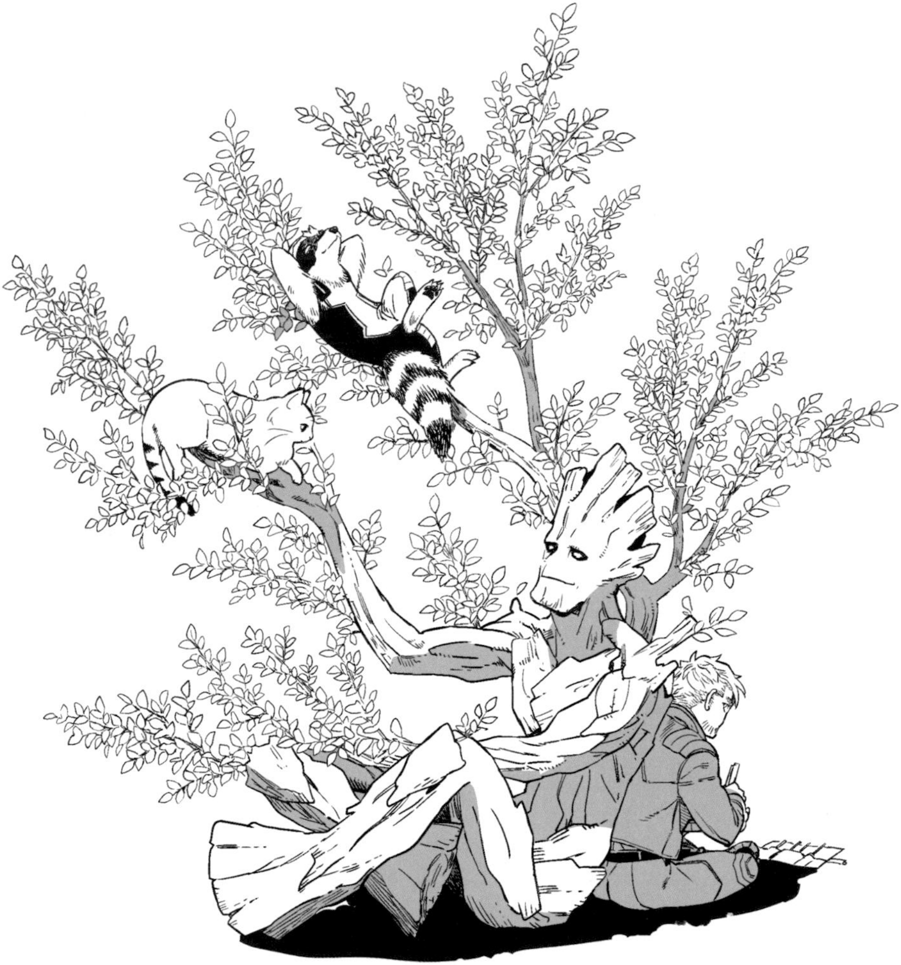

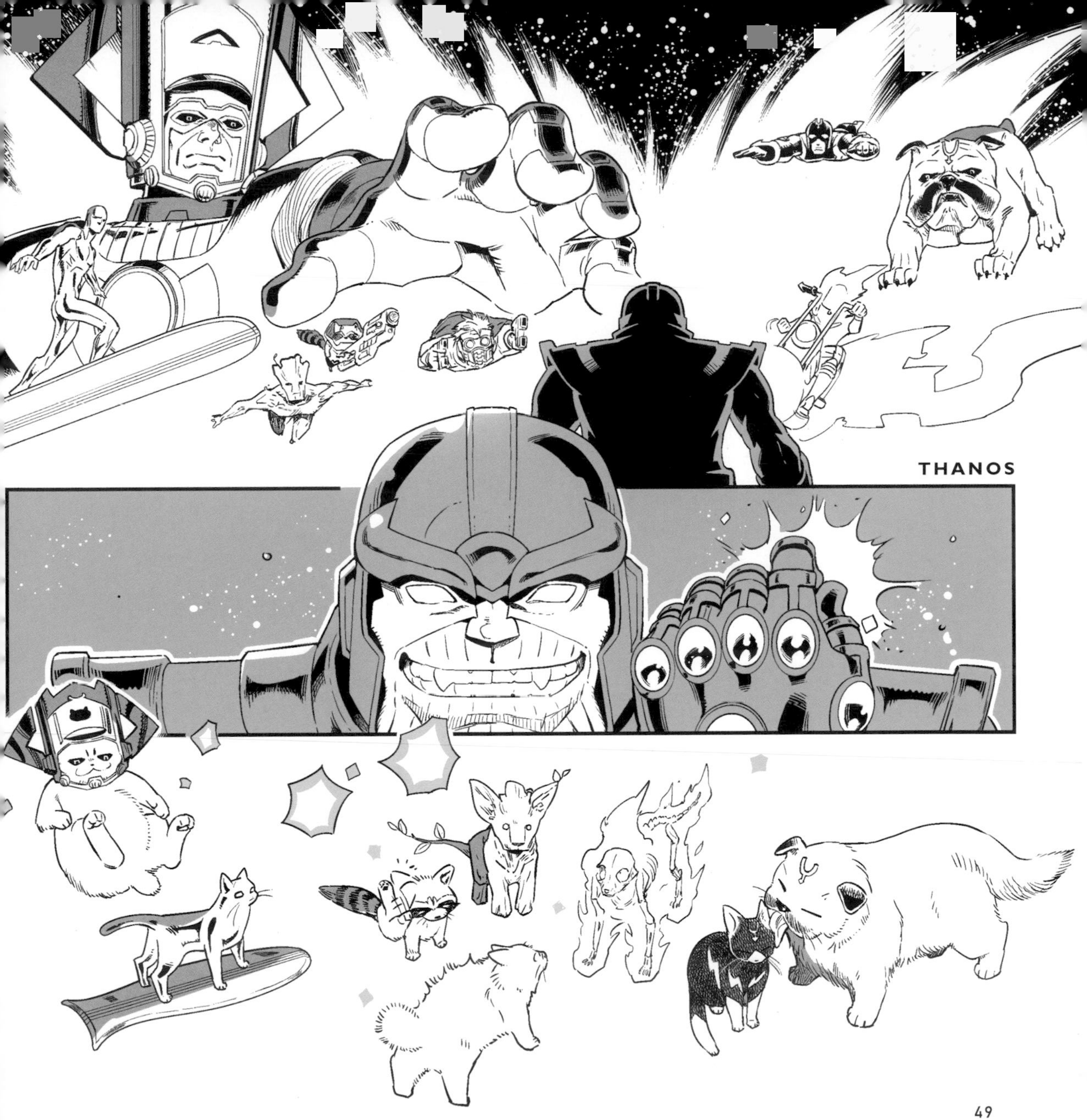
THANOS

# CHARACTER PROFILES

### MOON KNIGHT —— P35
Possesses multiple personalities, including another hero. Sometimes his personalities converse with each other.

### TASKMASTER —— P37
Able to mimic the movements of his opponents after seeing them only once. He is a talented mercenary and an excellent trainer.

### GHOST RIDER —— P39
His real name is Johnny Blaze. His Penance Stare makes his targets experience the suffering and pain they have inflicted on others.

### MEPHISTO —— P40
An arch-demon who collects souls by contracting with them. He made Blaze the Ghost Rider.

### SILVER SURFER —— P41
Wanders through space on his surfboard. He originally gained his powers as a herald of Galactus.

### GALACTUS —— P43
Driven by an endless hunger, Galactus is known as the Devourer of Worlds.

### GALACTA —— P43
Daughter of Galactus. Although she inherited her father's power, she is trying to live as a normal teenager on Earth.

## INHUMANS

### LOCKJAW —— P45
The pet dog of the Inhuman royal family. He can teleport.

### MEDUSA —— P45
Queen of the Inhumans. She has psychokinetic control over her long hair.

### CRYSTAL —— P45
Medusa's younger sister and a member of the Inhuman royal family. She can control the four elements of earth, water, fire, and air.

### KARNAK —— P45
A member of the Inhuman royal family. He is a martial arts master who can sense the weak point of any object or living thing.

### TRITON —— P45
A member of the Inhuman royal family. His superhuman powers are based on his aquatic mutation.

### MAXIMUS —— P45
Though he is a genius and at times has acted in his people's best interests, he covets his brother's throne.

### GORGON —— P45
A member of the Inhuman royal family. He can cause seismic shockwaves with his bull-like legs and hooves.

### BLACK BOLT —— P46
King of the Inhumans. Because of the destructive hypersonic power of his voice, he rarely speaks.

## GUARDIANS OF THE GALAXY

### GROOT —— P47
A treelike extraterrestrial sentient life-form who can sprout and grow limbs at will.

### ROCKET RACCOON —— P47
A master tactician and field commander who resembles a raccoon from Earth.

### PETER QUILL —— P48
Also known as Star-Lord. He is the founder of the Guardians of the Galaxy.

--------------------------------------------------

### THANOS —— P49
When Thanos wore the Infinity Gauntlet and gained the powers of a god, he was able to make all his wishes come true with the snap of his fingers.

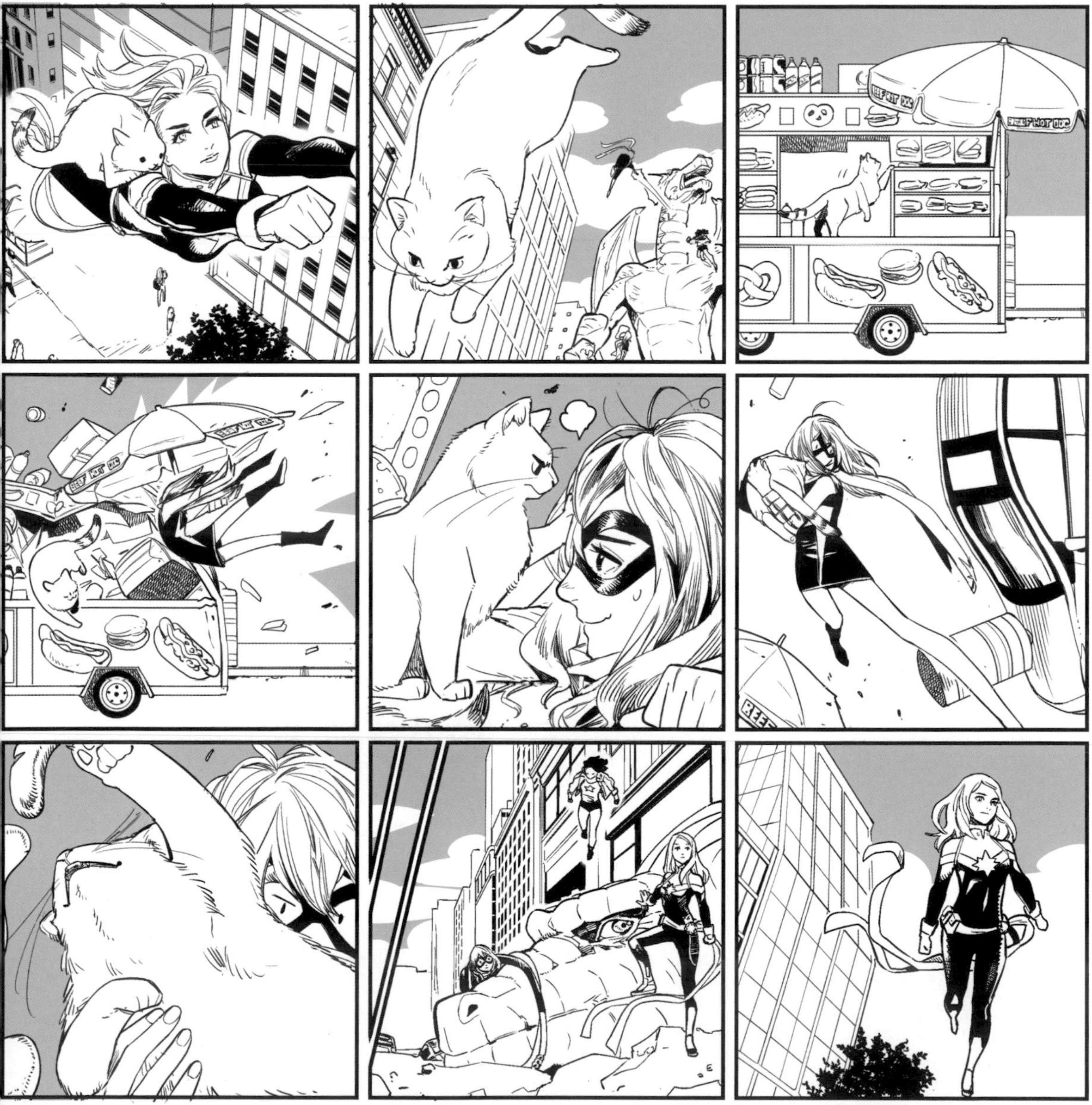
BEEF HOT DOG

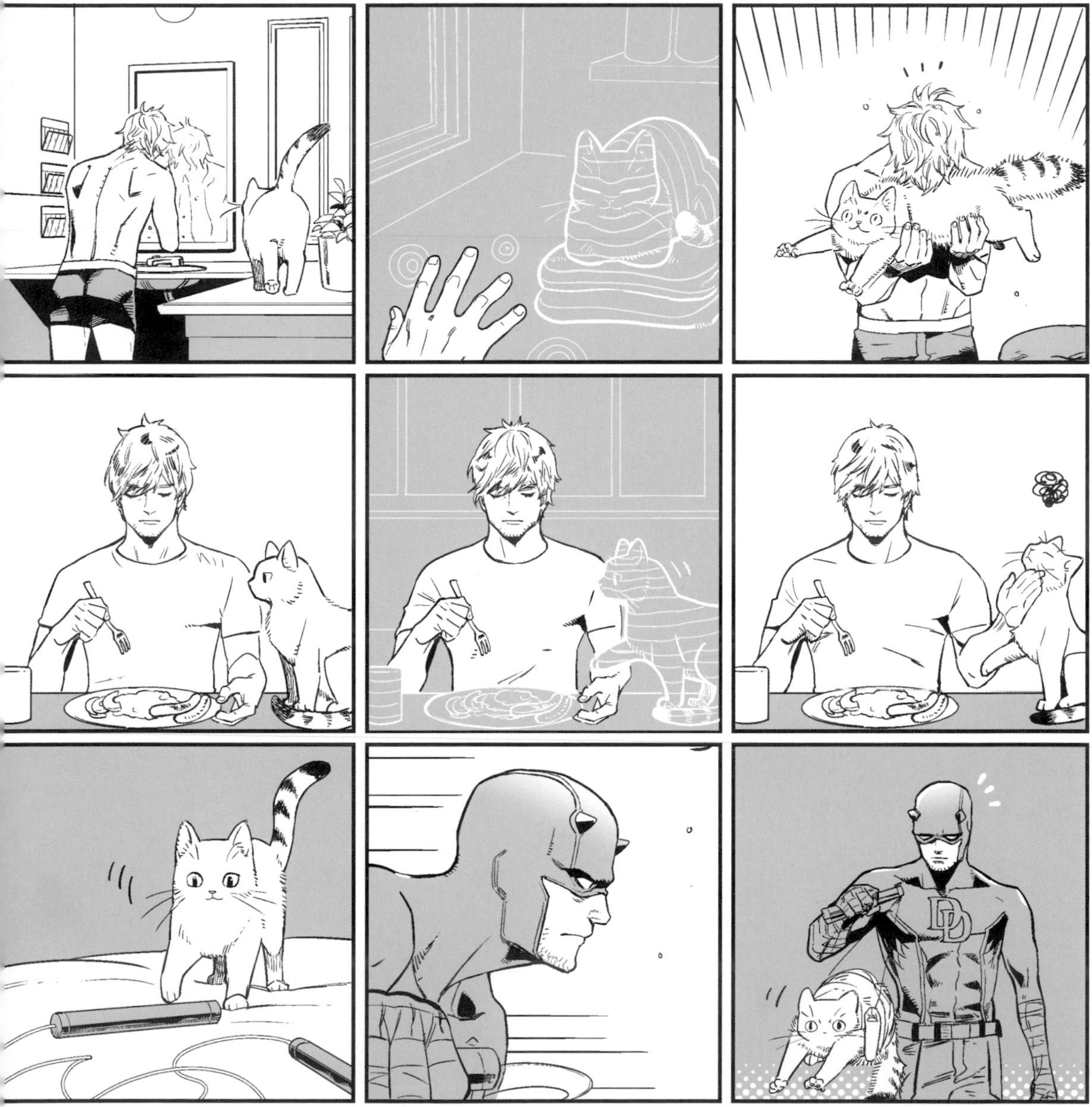

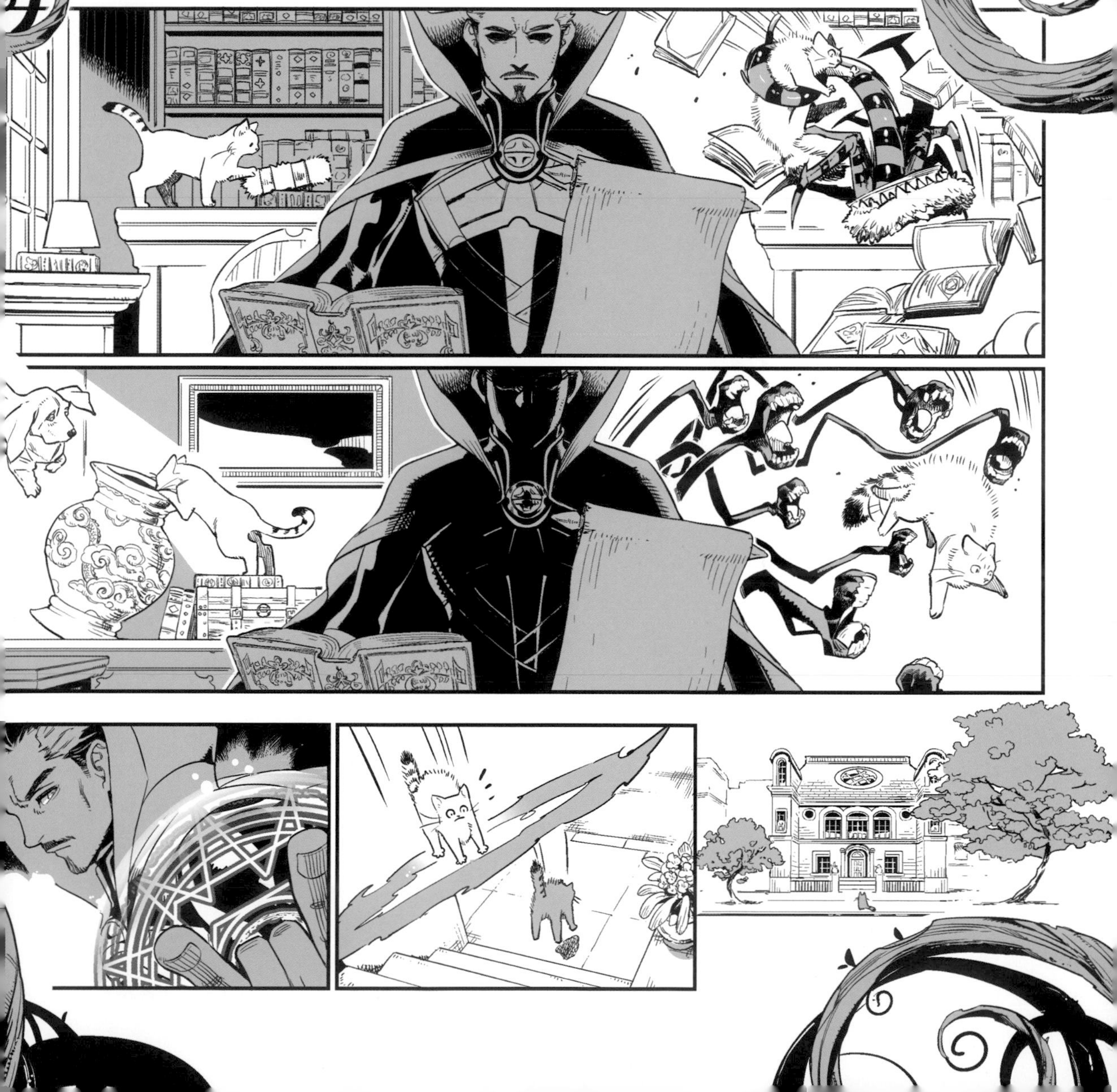

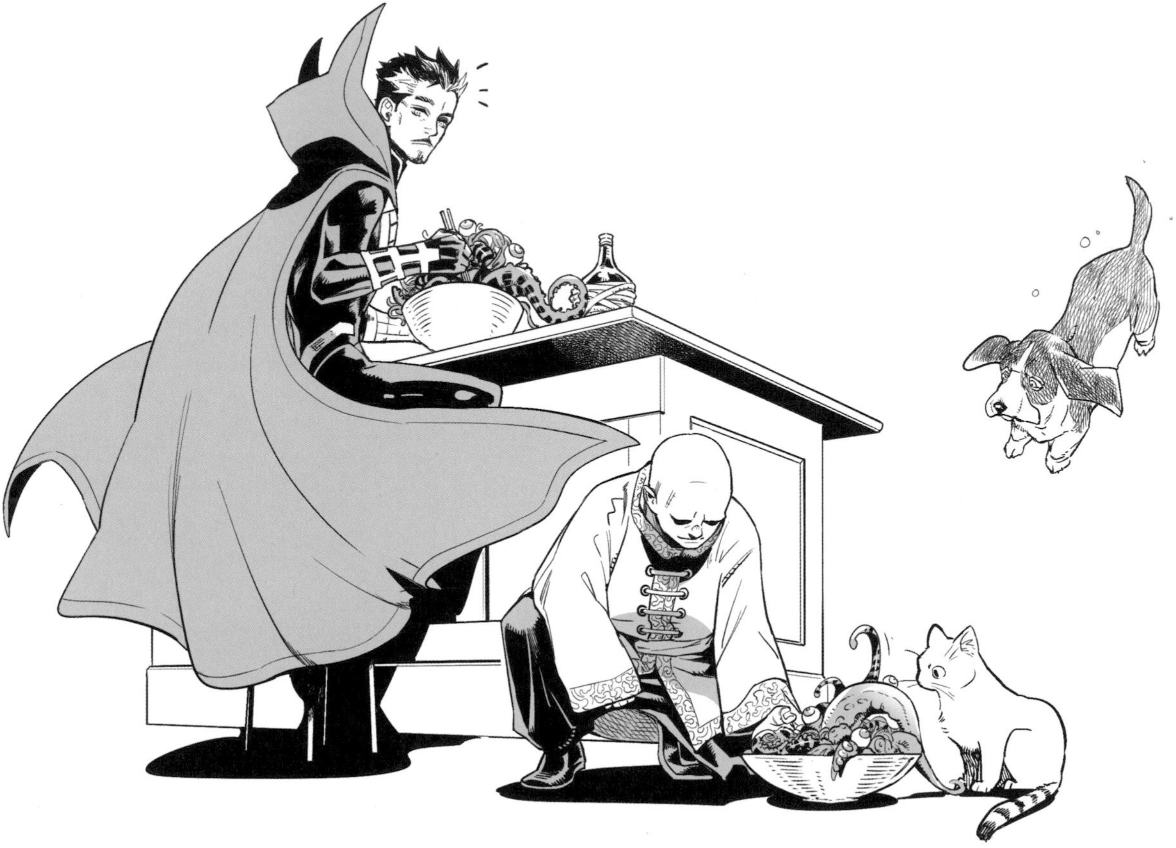

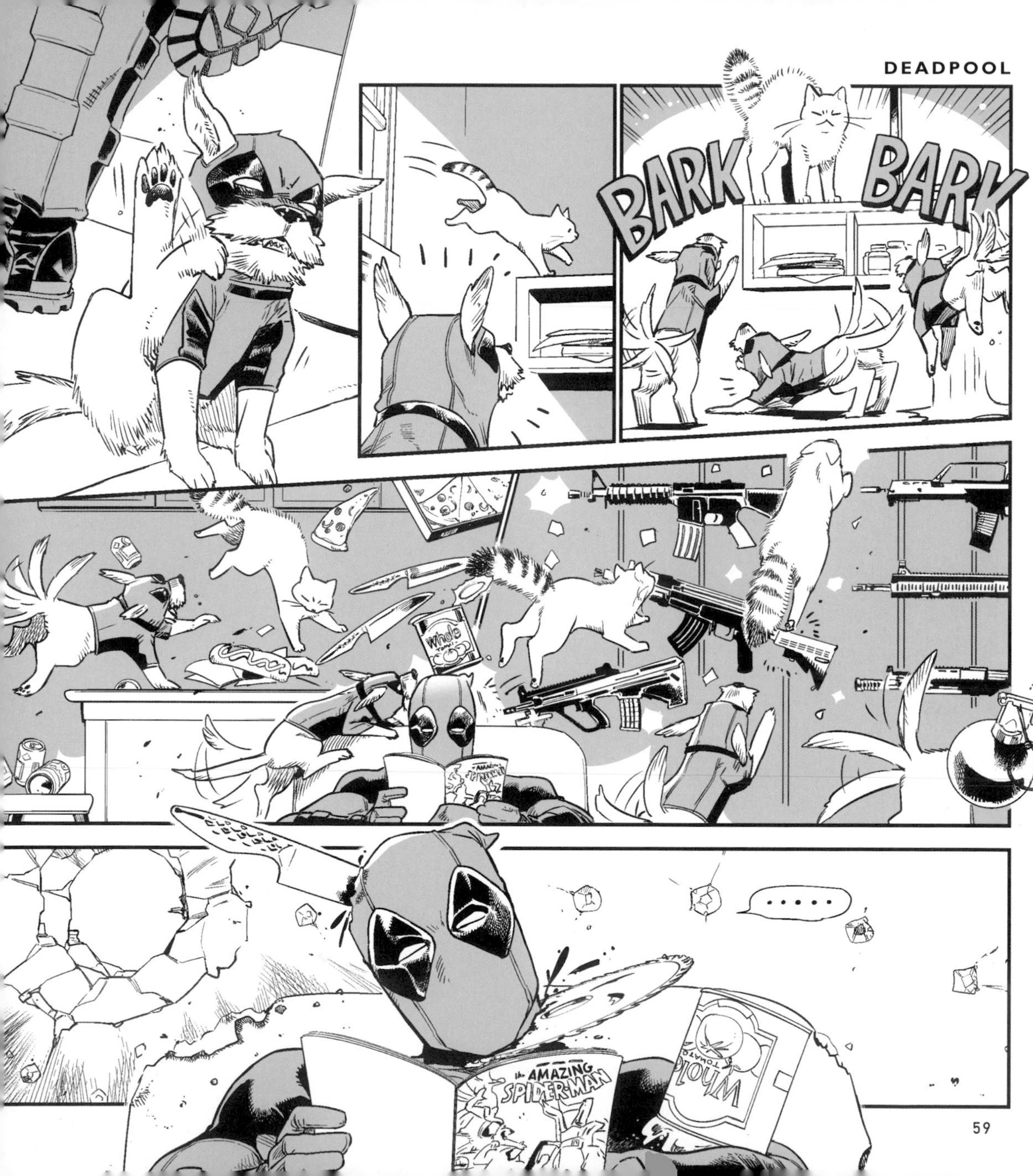
BARK BARK
......
whole TOMATO
the AMAZING SPIDER-MAN
whole TOMATO

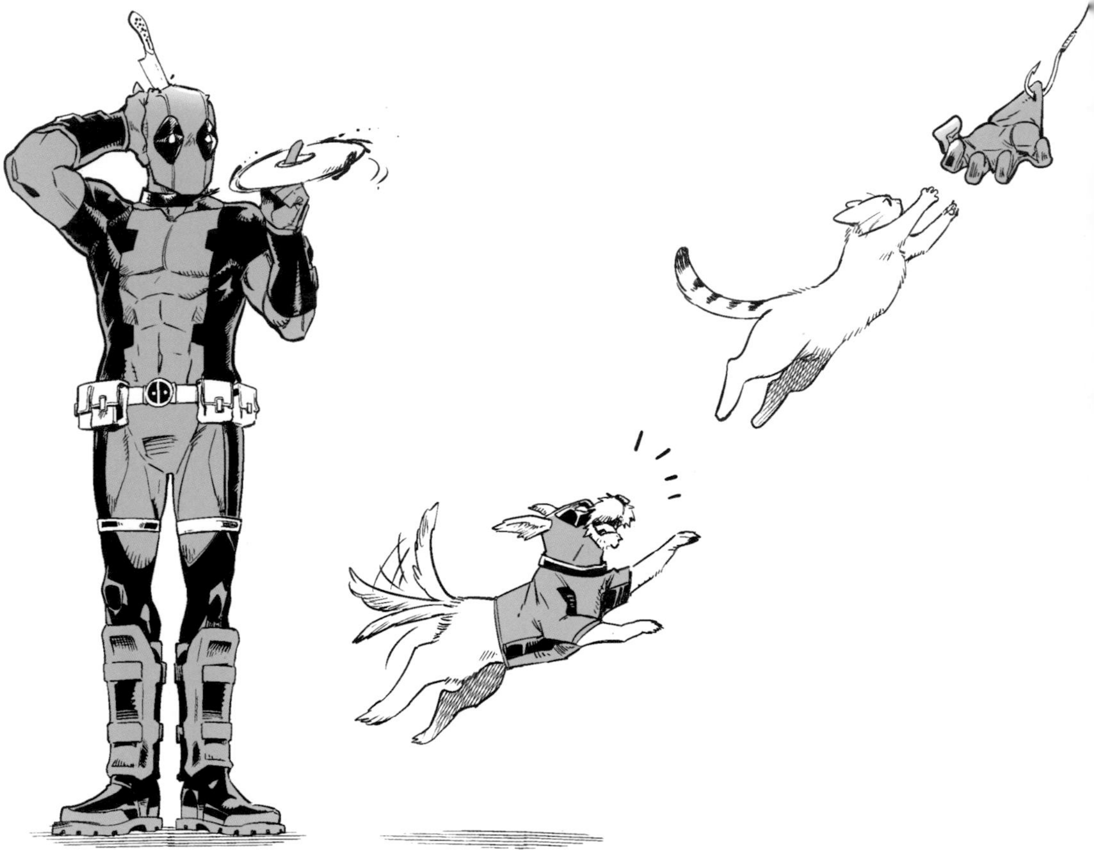

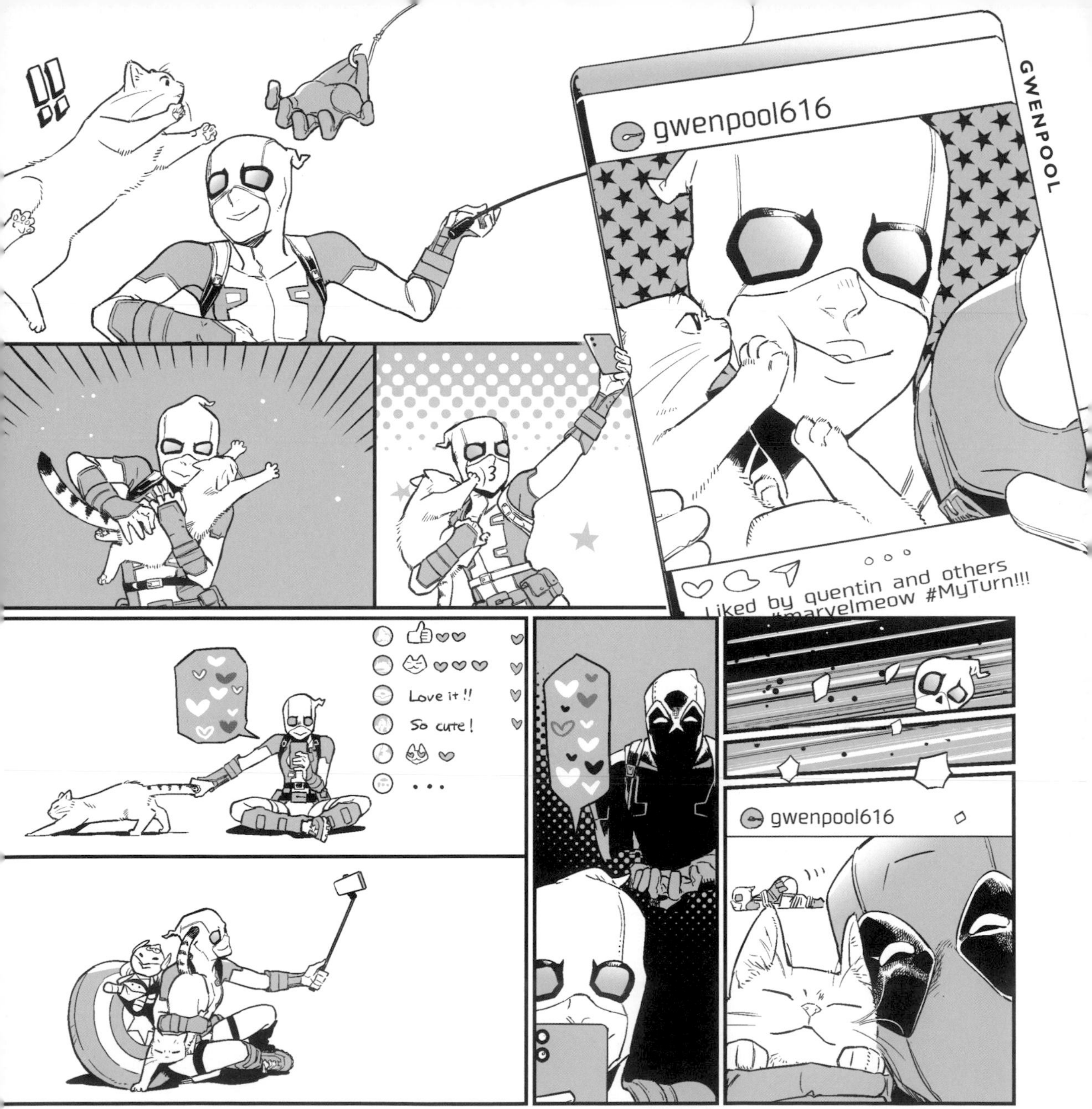
GWENPOOL
gwenpool616
Liked by quentin and others
#marvelmeow #MyTurn!!!
Love it !!
So cute !
gwenpool616

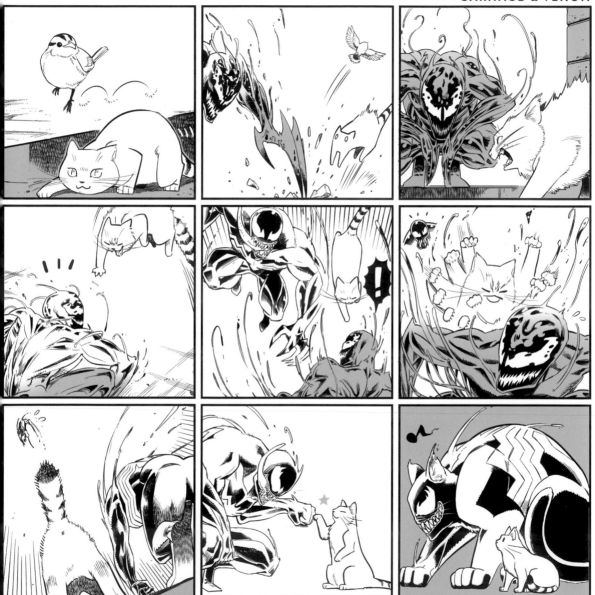

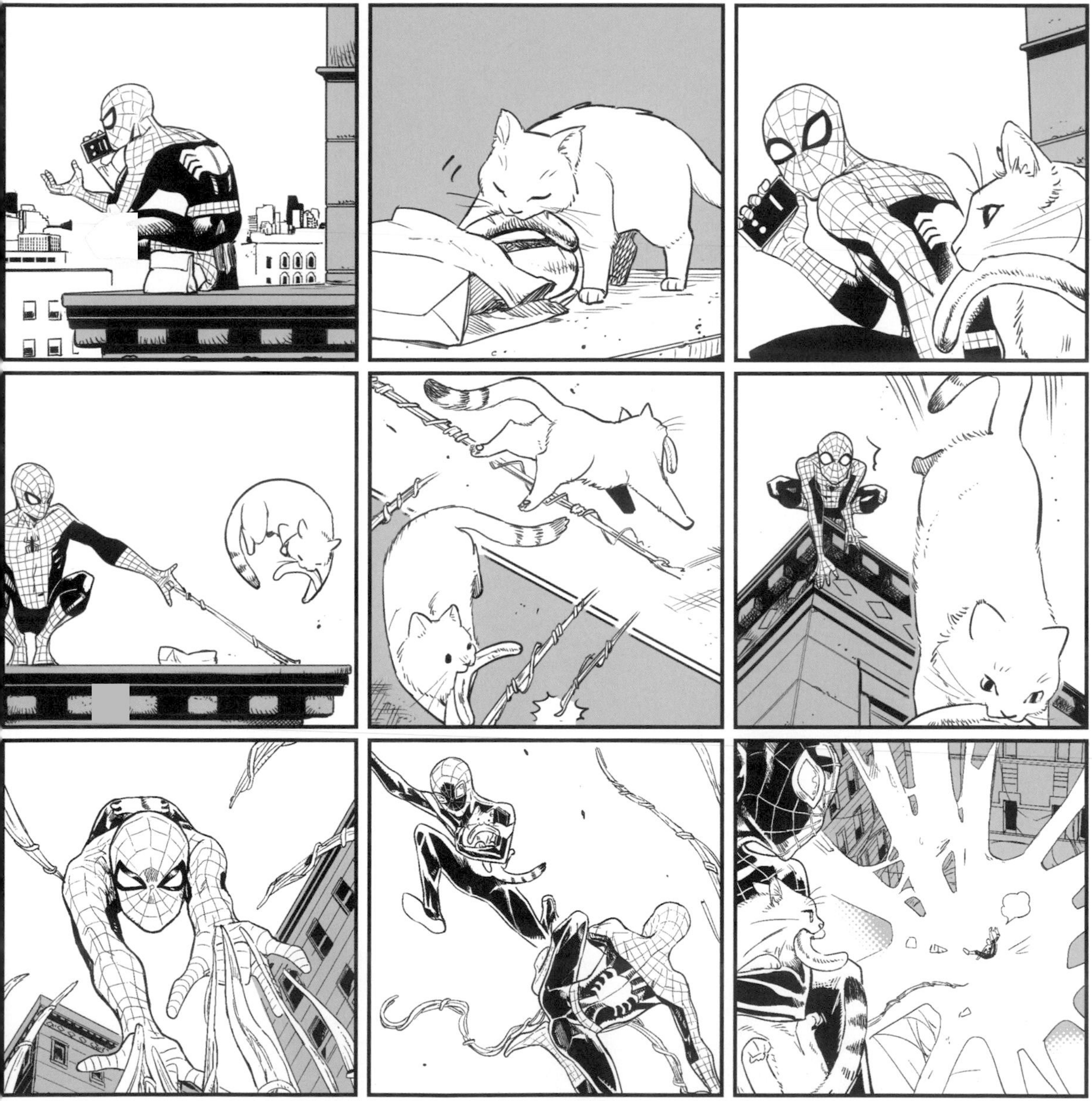

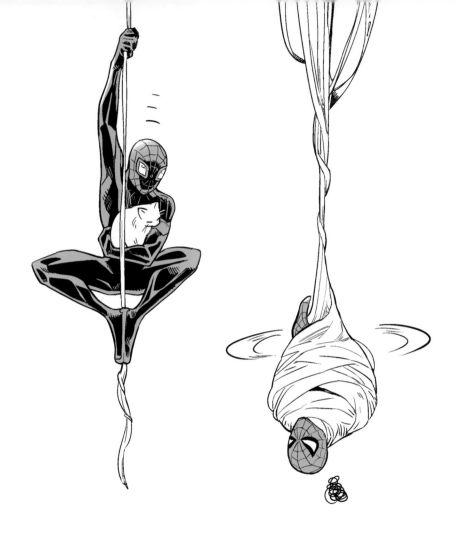

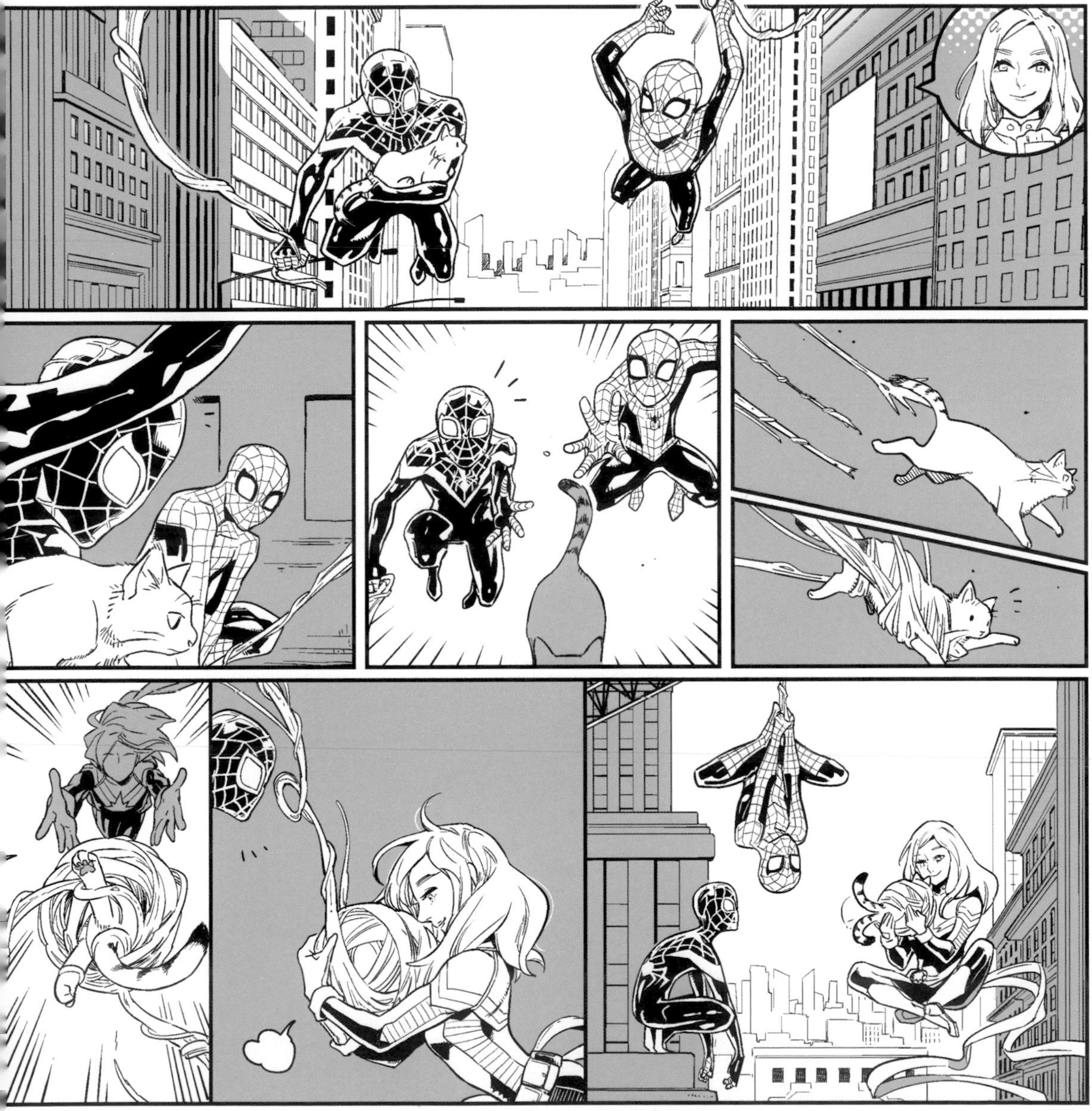

# CHARACTER PROFILES

## MS. MARVEL —— P53
Can change the shape of her body. She looks up to Captain Marvel.

## DAREDEVIL —— P55
Matt Murdock. Though he is blind, his other senses are superhuman. His weapon is a billy club with an extendable cable attached.

## DOCTOR STRANGE —— P57
The Sorcerer Supreme. His base, the Sanctum Sanctorum, stores magical books and tools. On the next page are his assistant Wong and Bats, a ghost dog who lives at the Sanctum.

## DEADPOOL —— P59
"The Merc with a Mouth." Deadpool has incredible regenerative healing abilities. Chasing Chewie is Dogpool, a dog version of Deadpool from an alternate universe.

## GWENPOOL —— P61
Believes she crossed into the world of comics from the "real world."

## VENOM —— P63
Venom was born when an alien Symbiote merged with a human host.

## CARNAGE —— P63
A vicious villain was created when a Symbiote bonded with a serial killer.

## SPIDER-MAN —— P65
Peter Parker. He gained superhuman powers when he was bitten by a radioactive spider.

## SPIDER-MAN —— P65
The Spider-Man in a black costume is Miles Morales. In an alternate universe, he was Peter Parker's successor.

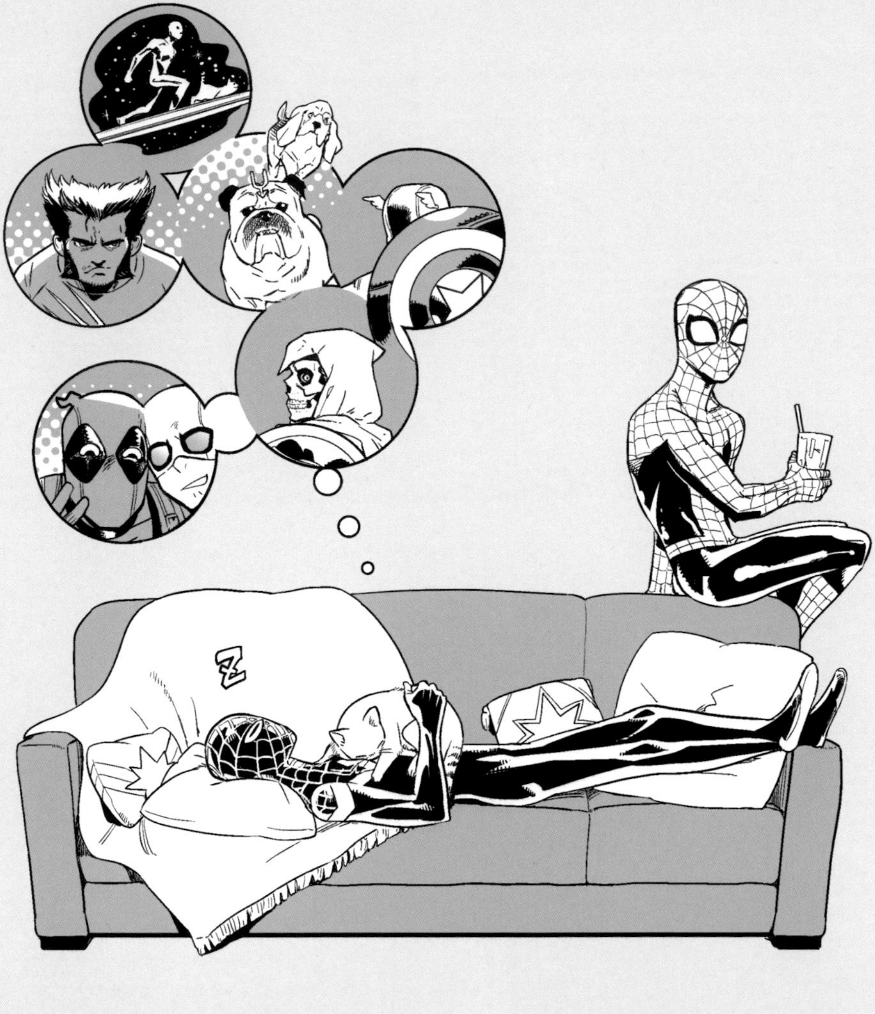
Z

**Nao Fuji**

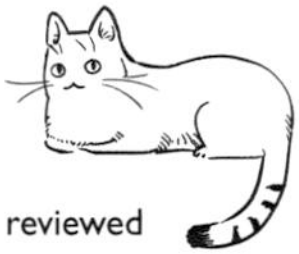

After having her portfolio reviewed at the first Tokyo Comic Con in 2016, Nao Fuji became an official Marvel artist with the release of *Marvel Meow*, a six-part comic series featuring Captain Marvel's pet, Chewie. Nao has also worked on short stories featuring Black Cat. She lives in Japan.

# MARVEL MEOW

VIZ MEDIA EDITION

## by Nao Fuji

TEXT BY **Shunsuke Nakazawa**

BOOK DESIGN, SHOGAKUKAN-SHUEISHA PRODUCTION EDITION  **Shinichi Sekine**
EDITOR, SHOGAKUKAN-SHUEISHA PRODUCTION EDITION  **Misato Sawada**

SENIOR EDITOR, VIZ MEDIA EDITION  **Amanda Ng**
DESIGNER, VIZ MEDIA EDITION  **Alice Lewis**

First published in Japan by Shogakukan-Shueisha Production Co., Ltd.

VIZ Media edition published by arrangement with Marvel Comics.

This edition published by
VIZ Media, LLC
P.O. Box 77010
San Francisco, CA 94107

Library of Congress Cataloging-in-Publication Data available.

10 9 8 7 6 5 4 3 2
First printing, October 2021
Second printing, October 2021

ISBN: 978-1-9747-2603-5

Printed in China

viz.com

© 2021 MARVEL